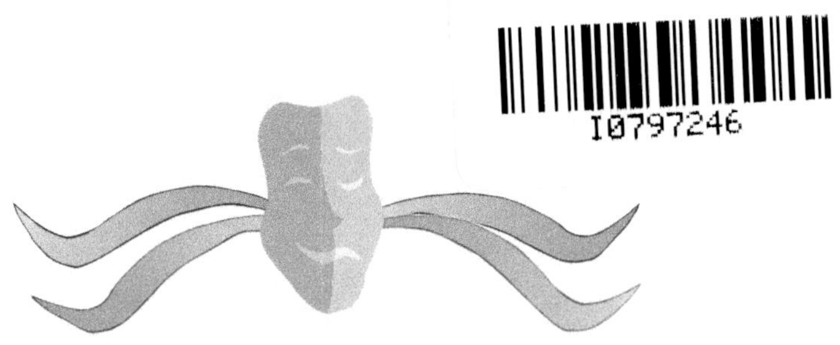

"Silverfoot's trembling. Something's wrong."
Thony looked at Amanita.
"Could it be wolves?"

The trees around them – which were already larger than any that the young prince had ever seen before – seemed to loom in and cut off the light filtering down through their leaves even more than they had been. That… had to be all his imagination, though… right? Even if his dapple-grey gelding, Silverfoot, was shaking from nose to tail.

Amanita looked around with an expression that was now shading over into concern. Her short, bushy hair flopped a little as she turned sharply from side to side, peering into the green shadows of the forest. Twinklestar, the unicorn she was riding, looked around with what might be equine trepidation as well.

"Can't Twinklestar *tell* you the problem?" Thony asked urgently, leaning forwards to try to give Silverfoot a better caress.

The girl shook her head, looking rather red around the ears. "We're not ***bonded,*** so I can't understand him in ***words.***"

If the unicorn was upset, Silverfoot was terrified. Thony was beginning to worry that the gelding's reaction would switch from half-paralyzed with fear to–

Oh, damn.

It was unfortunate that horses were trained to interpret a rider hunching into their backs as a signal to go *faster*. Because the only way to stay aboard a terrified horse that was plunging through a forest – instead of getting knocked off by low hanging branches – was to get as close as possible to the horse's back.

Thony had just barely the concentration left to hear Amanita's frustrated shout about this not being the right path.

Silverfoot wasn't following anything resembling a path.

THONY
GOES ASTRAY!

(in the deep, dark, and dangerous Fairy Wood)

Book Two of the Prankster Prince

KERRIDWEN MANGALA MCNAMARA

RISING DRAGON BOOKS

This book is a work of fiction. Names, characters, places, and incidents are the product of the author's imagination or are used fictitiously. Any resemblance to actual events, places or people, living or dead, is coincidental.

Also available in eBook and hardcover editions.
McNamara, Kerridwen Mangala
Thony Goes Astray! (in the Deep, Dark, and Dangerous Fairy Wood)/ by Kerridwen Mangala McNamara Indiana: Rising Dragon Books, 2023
p.
(McNamara, Kerridwen Mangala. The Prankster Prince; bk. 2)
Summary: Prince Thony, the stable-girl Amanita, and the unicorn Twinklestar make their way through the Fairy Wood to another world.
ISBN 978-1-960160-15-7 (pbk)
1. Princes and princesses - Fiction. 2. Adolescent Rebellion - Fiction
ISBN 978-1-960160-16-4 (hc) ISBN 978-1-960160-14-0 (eBook)

Thony and the Much-Anticipated Adventure: Book One of the Prankster Prince

Cover art and illustrations by the author
The Rising Dragon Logo was designed by Priyadevi McNamara

For further information, email RisingDragonBooks@gmail.com

ISBN: 978-1-960160-15-7
First Print Edition: September 2023
10 9 8 7 6 5 4 3 2 1

For Namita and Nandita Sugandhi:
Co-conspirators in writing in our ‘days of eld.’

And for my kids...
who kept insisting I get started on this.

CONTENTS

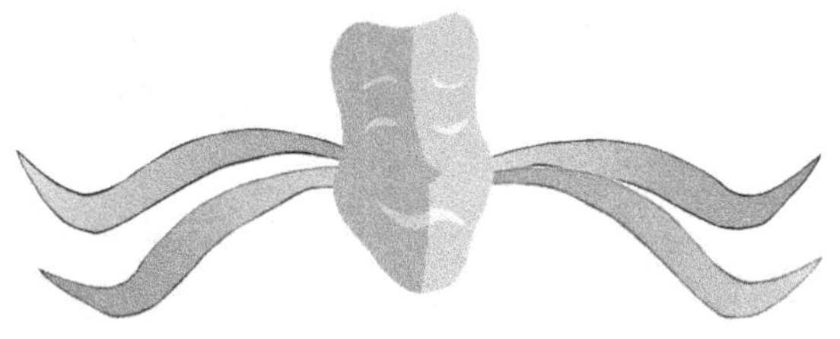

Chapter ONE

The Adventure Begins… *Grumpy*

RUNNING AWAY FROM HOME FOR all the right reasons should be a great deal less *annoying*, Thony thought to himself as he guided his handsome, dapple-grey gelding along behind Amanita on the unicorn, Twinklestar. None of the stories he'd eked out of travelers – or any of the books he'd read – had mentioned all these *annoying* parts.

For one thing, *dew* was not just something that looked pretty and sparkly if one got up early enough to see it on all the grass and spiderwebs and things. It apparently dampened your clothes nearly as badly as if it had been raining. And wet clothes were a definite downer.

For another, dry cheese and hardtack tasted even worse than they sounded. And eating them a-saddle didn't help *at all*.

And *then* there was the 'company'. Though, presumably, some people had more choice of traveling companions and didn't get stuck with a bossy little girl on a grumpy unicorn.

To be fair, Amanita had followed him into his escape without any hesitation *(or being asked)* simply because she knew, firsthand, how very dangerous was the place he was going. And she knew that because she'd somehow traversed the Fairy Wood herself *(though with advice or directions or something from someone named 'Quellarie')*. And she'd done it with no warning from Thony that he was leaving, no plan or preparation... and she was taking him back to her homeworld, even though she didn't particularly want to go back.

It was the act of a true friend, and he'd known that Amanita had definitely been one of Thony's best friends even before she'd demonstrated it so thoroughly.

But Oh. My. God. did she have to be so *annoyingly superior* about how much more she knew about using the Fairy Wood to travel between worlds than he did? *(Or even just plain traveling than he did...)*

He'd almost rather try this alone than have to listen to another rant about how unprepared he was.

Well, no. No, he wouldn't. Not if there really *were* lava worlds and poison gas worlds and worlds full of *carnivorous plant people* that one might run into simply by going the wrong way around a specific tree in the Fairy Wood. And having a native guide to her homeworld was probably a good idea, too. *(Assuming her homeworld didn't have even worse things. Or maybe especially if it* **did***, since it seemed he was going to be going there.)*

But, seriously? They hadn't been riding for a full hour yet, and he *was* doing everything she said. Couldn't the pint-sized girl lay off on giving him a lecture every time he asked a simple question?

Thony was beginning to think that Amanita really must come from a matriarchal culture, the way she'd always said, and he hadn't believed. *(Because,* ***girls?*** *Running a* ***country?*** *How wack-a-doodle was* ***that?****)* She certainly didn't seem to think a boy could do anything without screwing it up... though she hadn't seemed to have this much of an attitude when she was working as a kitchen-girl and then a stable-girl back in Aldyrwald.

Where Thony was better known as Crown Prince Anthony Devinthal, the Affable and the Affirmative. *Of Aldyrwald.*

He hadn't cared much about his title then – it was a burden as much as anything.

If not for his title, Thony would have been free to make friends with the village kids, or at least the squires.

If not for his title, Thony would have been allowed to learn swordplay and archery and how to make a fire and maybe gotten to travel *(before forcing the issue this way).*

If not for his title, Thony wouldn't have had to flee home into the *deep, dark, and dangerous Fairy Wood* to spare his parents from having to make him marry an elderly princess while he was almost underage himself in hopes of averting a region-wide war that would surely shred Aldyrwald into itty, bitty, bloody little pieces.

Now, however, he found himself clinging to the stupid thing to remind himself that a Prince did not succumb to taunts and snarky comments from a pipsqueak of a commoner girl. A Prince used his Manners and was always Kind and Generous in Thought and Action with those of lesser birth. A Prince should be *Grateful* for the assistance his guide was providing... no matter how obnoxiously it was offered.

Perhaps making that last part clear would help. *(Or the second-to-last, anyways.)* Though he thought he'd already said it before – one of the few pieces of advice his father, King Bill, had given Thony in the Ways of Women had been that you could never tell them positive things too often.

"Hey, Amanita," he called out. "Thanks again for coming along like this. I really appreciate you offering to guide me through the Fairy Wood."

"And well you should be," came back the snarky reply. "You have *no idea* what you were getting yourself into here."

With a manful effort, Thony did *not* grind his teeth so hard that she'd be able to hear it.

"It can't be *that* bad," he heard himself saying before he managed to censor the thought. "Joanna and Priscilla and Roger managed the feat just last year. *Without* a guide of any sort."

A snort of derision came from ahead. "Yeah, and the Perushin tail Princess Priscilla has had *nothing* to do with that, of course. *Or* the fact that the three of them were destined to come back and be the new Gods of your world after they found their counterparts."

That still sent a little bit of a chill up Thony's spine when Amanita said it so nonchalantly as all that. Joanna and Roger had thought – as best he could tell – that they were taking the devastated Priscilla on a husband-hunting Quest, or a Quest to find out *why* and *how* the otherwise perfectly princessly maiden had a bushy, black, prehensile tail that was almost as long as she was tall. And maybe, just *maybe,* to find a way to make their own hopelessly ill-starred romance work out.

They certainly *hadn't* been expecting to discover a not-so-evil Wizard and Sorceress holed up in an extinct volcano on another world who were apparently *waiting* for them because Cythera had been having dreams that she and Phillip were supposed to Save the World, except it wasn't *their* world, it was *Thony's* world that they were supposed to Save. And to be told by the Fairy Queen herself that the way they were supposed to Save it was by *becoming* the next set of Gods – along with Roger and Joanna and Priscilla – when all the *old* Gods of that world died in some dramatic thing called a 'Ragnarök'.

And the Fairy Queen had married Roger and Joanna to each other. And Phillip and Cythera. And Priscilla and her centaur boyfriend Jeremy as well.

And then they'd all come back home and Mama and Papa had made Roger and Joanna have a *second* wedding 'for propriety's sake' *(i.e., to show the neighbors that they really were married)* and then the 'Ragnarök' had happened. Joanna had become Goddess of Earth and a mountain – Her *Holy* Mountain – had appeared and enveloped the back half of the Devinthals' castle. And Roger had disappeared for a few weeks; He was now the God of Air and had a perpetual Holy Tornado spinning on the exact opposite side of the world, He told them. Phillip was now God of Water and Cythera was Goddess of Fire, and They had disappeared off to other places to do Their God-Stuff, and had only come by for a few hours for the wedding. Priscilla had become Goddess of Love and Animals *(the former title apparently being a euphemism as much as anything and explained the overlap with the second one, but Mama and Papa –* **and Thony** *– appreciated the euphemism).*

Mama and Papa were still trying to pretend Priscilla and Jeremy weren't *really* married. Though since Thony had spilled the beans to Papa yesterday about Priscilla turning herself into a centaur-girl when she was out running with Jeremy and his herd... maybe that would help? Eventually? At least after Mama had a chance to faint over it a few times.

Thony hadn't heard that the intrepid Questers had figured anything out about Prissy's tail, though it was possible that he'd just missed the explanation in all the commotion that had included two rather upset pairs of parents planning an emergency wedding and trying to make it look pre-planned and Roger's father nearly disowning him and Mama and Papa refusing to acknowledge Jeremy and having screaming matches with the sweet and agreeable Priscilla. Not to mention that the neighbors didn't believe any of the Ragnarök/new-God stuff and Papa feared they were going to claim that the Devinthals had lost the Divine Right of Kings and use that as an excuse to invade Aldyrwald and take it over.

Which came back to why he'd run away.

"What do you mean about Prissy's tail?" he demanded. How could *Amanita* know about this if *he* didn't?

"Perushin have all their magick in their tails," Amanita explained in a patronizing tone. "The tails give them luck and grant their wishes; they don't actually have to do *formal* magick at all since anything they *want* just sort of *happens*. Newborns receive a tail from an elderly one who's passing away, and the magick gets stronger with every generation. When one of their tails somehow goes astray, it's a Big Deal with them. Like your sister's."

"And you know this, *how?*" Thony said skeptically. Or, at least, he was trying to sound skeptical. He had no better explanation for Prissy's tail himself, after all. But it sounded made-up. He'd never heard of these 'Perushin' things before.

Amanita gave him one of those superior looks over her shoulder. "I spent a few days in the Perushin village on my way to Aldyrwald."

Hunh. He could have sworn that she'd said her mysterious mentor had given her directions to *his* world. And that it wasn't wise to take detours in the–

"You went *exploring* in the Fairy Wood, didn't you," he realized. "Even though you'd been told not to. And these Perushin things had to set you properly on your way again."

Her superior expression converted instantly to a scowl. "It wasn't exactly on purpose."

Twinklestar, the unicorn she was riding, snorted a little.

Something eased in Thony's chest. "Uh-hunh. Right."

Her lips pursed. "And I suppose you think you could do better, Prince Smarty-Pants. Without *any* instruction at all."

The young prince put on a pious expression. "I didn't say that. I just said I was grateful for your help, didn't I?"

Silverfoot curvetted a little and Thony adjusted his grip on the reins. He patted the dapple-grey's neck soothingly.

"Look, *dude*–"

Amanita's irritated comment was cutoff as Twinklestar came to an abrupt, stiff-legged halt and Silverfoot actually bumped into him before stopping as well.

"Twinkie, what the hell–" Amanita began, but Thony cut her off.

"Silverfoot's trembling. Something's wrong." He looked at the girl. "Could it be wolves?"

The trees around them – which were already larger than any he had ever seen before – seemed to loom in and cut off the light filtering down through their leaves even more than they had been. That... had to be all his imagination, though... right?

Amanita looked around with an expression that was now shading over into concern. Her short, bushy hair flopped a little as she turned sharply from side to side, peering into the green shadows of the forest.

"Can't he *tell* you the problem?" Thony asked urgently, leaning forwards to try to give Silverfoot a better caress.

The girl shook her head, looking rather red around the ears. "We're not *bonded,* so I can't understand him in *words.*"

"He talks to *Prissy* in words," the young prince objected. "And *they're* not bonded."

Amanita gave him a dark glare. "Look, *I* don't get words from him. Maybe *you* can convince him to tell you why. In *words*. All I know right now is that he's upset. And that's easy to see from body-language."

If the unicorn was upset, Silverfoot was *terrified*. Thony was beginning to worry that the gelding's reaction would switch from half-paralyzed with fear to–

Oh, damn.

It was unfortunate that horses were trained to interpret a rider hunching into their backs as a signal to go *faster*. Because the only way to stay aboard a terrified horse that was plunging through a forest – instead of getting knocked off by low hanging branches – was to get as close as possible to the horse's back.

Thony had just barely the concentration left to hear Amanita's frustrated shout about this not being the right path. Silverfoot wasn't following anything resembling a *path*.

It was the most terrifying handful of minutes of the young prince's *(admittedly sheltered and overly protected)* life.

At last, however, the dapple-grey's terror lost out to the extreme effort necessary to keep forcing his way at high speed through thickets and brambles. He came to a trembling stop in a glade alongside a small stream, his head hanging down and panting.

Thony kind of felt like hanging his head down and panting as well. Not to mention how much *he* was trembling. He more or less slithered off of Silverfoot's back rather than properly dismounting, and stumbled over to the stream to put some water on his face.

The horse followed, to take a drink.

After a moment, Thony sat back on his heels on the mossy streambank, regarding his extremely-goodlooking-but-apparently-thickwitted horse with rather less enthusiasm than he'd begun with. He'd been so excited when the stablemaster had taken pity on him and found a way to trick Great-Uncle Sir Eddie into thinking switching Thony onto this gelding had been the old knight's own idea *(and then Great-Uncle Sir Eddie had convinced Mama and Papa...)*. Silverfoot had seemed to be an improvement over the nearly somnolent mare, Rosie, that he'd recently been moved up to from the aged pony he'd been riding since he'd been eight...

...but right now, Rosie was sounding better and better. Even if she'd panicked like this, she wouldn't have managed to go nearly so far.

Oh, well. If it was his old *pony* he'd absconded on, likely the elderly equine would have just died of fright, leaving Thony on foot to face whatever the problem was.

Not really better.

Maybe.

Amanita had managed to convince him that the Fairy Wood was not a safe place to go exploring in. Going the wrong way around certain trees could apparently end you up in very different places. You had to stick *exactly* to known paths, she claimed. *(Although the recent conversation suggested there might be more flex in that concept than she'd insisted.)*

Well, *that* idea was clearly out the window.

He was lost and alone – except for his idiot horse – barely an hour's ride into the Fairy Wood.

Silverfoot gave him what might have been a sheepish look for a human and nosed at the seated boy. Out of habit, Thony scratched the usual itchy places on the large head, his heart softening.

"You did what made sense to you, didn't you, boy?" he muttered to Silverfoot. "Not your fault if this wasn't the place to follow your instincts. And... who knows what scared you so bad anyways. Maybe staying would have been worse."

Which was all fine and dandy, but now he'd lost Amanita. So, he had no guide, as well as not having done a particularly stellar job of taking care of his friend; who knew what she and the unicorn had been faced with after Silverfoot galloped off?

Not to mention that she would never let him live this down, if he ever managed to find her again.

And if the Fairy Wood was as *deep, dark and dangerous* as she'd told him – and as impossible to retrace one's path in – Thony was in even more trouble than that. Even outside of the issues of navigating in a place this tricksy, he had close to zero survival skills. He *had* a tinderbox and flint-striker with him, for example, but he'd never built an actual fire and only knew how to get a useful spark because of having to light the occasional candle and for a set of pranks a few years ago that had not gone terribly well *(fire tended to get out of control, as he'd discovered the hard way, and a good prank should always be completely under the prankster's control, in his opinion).*

Well. Breaking down big problems into smaller ones was the way to plan out a good prank. It would likely help here, too. Problem One, was immediate survival, but he and Silverfoot weren't injured and it wasn't even mid-day yet, so that wasn't actually urgent. Problem Two, was safely navigating the Fairy Wood to a reasonable location where he could look for a princess. Important, but also not urgent. Problem Three, was finding Amanita and keeping her safe until he could get her back to her home... or possibly to Aldyrwald, since Thony was fairly sure their mutual friend and co-prankster, Wesley, was sweet on her.

Possibly he had Problems Two and Three reversed, but there seemed to be abundant sub-problems mixed in as part of each of them...

Which he should likely try to divide up more finely, given that he *still* had no idea what to do next...

"Girona, this way! I think we found them!"

He looked up in surprise at the cheerful voice, just in time to see a girl of about his own age come out of the thicket of trees on the other side of the stream. Long, dark hair, skin that looked tanned, but wearing a long, white gown of some sort. None of the noblewomen *he* knew would wear a gown that bared their arms and shoulders, nor allow their skin to become so tanned. But no commoner would ever even try to manage a floor-length gown of such a perfect, crystalline white. And certainly not in a forest.

As he frowned, trying to figure the girl out, another one partially emerged from the trees behind her.

This one was shorter, with hair that was up in a nice-looking messy bun, and wearing more of a tunic-and-pants outfit in – he had to blink at the colors – *lavender and chartreuse.* Some sort of magickal-ish looking symbols seemed to be sewn onto it. She was also too well-dressed to be a commoner.

"There's only the one kid, Midele," the shorter girl complained. "You said there would be two of them."

The taller girl shrugged. "Maybe I was wrong. This is the boy from the vision anyways. I also thought that you'd simply be drawn to your mirror-self, but *you* thought it was wiser to make the compass. And it was the compass that got us *here.*"

"It was, wasn't it." The shorter girl's face was still mostly in the shadows, but she looked rather insufferably smug, and the taller one rolled her eyes. "I should have come to visit you guys in Quest'sEnd *ages* ago. Nothing this interesting ever happens at home."

Thony had climbed to his feet and put a hand warily on his horse as he watched the pair approach. They seemed harmless or even friendly, but he had nowhere safe to flee if they were actually ogres in disguise or something, and Amanita's stories had him pretty paranoid by now. "Um, hello?"

The taller girl came forwards out of the shadows of the trees. She was pretty, he supposed, but not dazzling or anything.

"Hi," she returned. "I'm Midele Featherspray, and this is my cousin, Girona Starshine. I'm from Flowericka on the world of Eyola, and Girona is from a country called Happy-Go-Lucky. Who are you?"

This 'Midele' seemed to take it for granted that they might be from different worlds than him. Which said something right there. If he could only figure out *what.*

"I'm... Thony," the young prince replied. No need for titles until and unless he really did find his princess, after all. "I'm from Aldyrwald... That's my country. I don't know if my world has a name. It isn't common knowledge at home that there *are* any other worlds."

"Oh, it's not common knowledge on Eyola either," Midele said easily. "But I'm a novice priestess of the Golden Sphinx and Girona is a student wizard. What do you do?"

The other girl spared him from having to answer. "Does it *matter,* Midele? We were supposed to find two of them, and there's only the one. Maybe you're wrong about this part, too, and he's not the kid you had the vision about."

Thony gave the taller girl a raised eyebrow. "You had a *vision* about me?"

She blushed slightly in a way that looked entirely unplanned – not like Mama's ladies-in-waiting, who practiced their blushes regularly.

"It sounds a little silly to just say it straight up like that. It's... part of a meditation practice I've been learning as a novice priestess. Occasionally the Golden Sphinx grants us a vision. Usually, it's of something we're supposed to do. In this case, I saw myself and Girona meeting up with a girl who looks enough like her to be a twin – and a redheaded boy with a silver horse." She nodded at Silverfoot. "There was supposed to be a white unicorn also – and Girona said that *they* never come out into Eyola, so we knew we had to go into the Fairy Wood."

The shorter girl stepped out of the shadows, and Thony could see that she did, indeed, look like a perfect copy of Amanita. Well, except for the um, *assertively* messy hair and the outrageous clothes. He couldn't have imagined his friend looking like this; Amanita was absolutely obsessed with neatness and seemed allergic to bright colors... though the last might simply have been because she'd always been wearing work clothes while he'd known her.

This girl looked like she took a sort of obscure pride in 'not caring' what other people thought of her while she intentionally startled them.

"My horse panicked – I'm not sure why," Thony admitted. "He ran off and we lost my friend who looks like you," he added, looking pointedly at Girona.

"Hunh," the other girl even *sounded* like Amanita in a good mood, now that he was paying attention. "So, the compass worked after all. That is, I assume you set it to point to him and not to *her*, Midele," she said in an irritatingly *knowing* sort of way.

Midele rolled her eyes again. "Of course, I did. The other girl should be your mirror-self from another world. I thought you'd be automatically drawn to each other, so we wouldn't need any more of a guide than that. I thought the compass was overkill, if you recall."

"*'Mirror-self'?*" Thony asked, beginning to be interested.

Midele started to smile at him, but Girona spoke first. "A lot of people have *'analogues'* on other worlds. Someone who is just like you, but born somewhere else. Midi's using the popular term. Since she's not a *specialist,* like *me.*"

The taller girl shot Girona a dark look. "You're a wizard *student,* Gronie, not a *specialist* in otherworldly travels. Not *yet,* anyways," she added in what sounded like a mollifying tone.

Girona shrugged. "Fine, *Midele.*" She looked at Thony again and added in almost as condescending a tone, "There's some evidence to suggest that *mirror-selves* are ubiquitous – everyone has one *some*where. And some wizards have hypothesized that there can be *more* than one, or that they can even appear on the *same* world. No one has proven that yet, though. And I don't get to the classes on Alchemical Proofs for another couple of years," she admitted.

"It shouldn't seem hard to prove those things," Thony objected. "Don't you just need to find someone with multiple analogues or two of them born on the same world?"

She somehow looked down her nose at him, despite being half a foot shorter. The slope of the land might have helped; they were on the higher bank of the stream. The trees were smaller on that side, too. "There are more people on any given world than I think *you* can *comprehend.* And very, very few of them do any world-hopping. It's a harder problem than you might think. What we're looking for is a *theoretical* proof."

"Hmmn." Thony had grazed the ideas of mathematical proofs in his studies. It had sounded interesting, but more abstract than his tutor – the Minister of Aldyrwald's tiny treasury – really understood himself, so the young prince had only the slightest idea of what such things were all about.

Midele shook her head, that long hair – knee-length at least – swishing back and forth as she did so. "The other girl should be attracted to you here, then, Girona. Maybe the point of my vision was for us to help the two of them find each other again–"

"Eeeew!" Girona's reaction was about what Amanita's would have been to that implication. Or Thony's own, actually, so he didn't feel a need to take umbrage.

"– so that they can navigate the Fairy Wood together. If they want to end up in the same place, that's the only way to do it, after all. *Honestly,* Girona." Midele shook her head again. "Just call the picnic basket, why don't you, and let's have something to eat."

She started to bunch up her skirts in preparation to wade the stream, and Thony was startled to see that the novice priestess was barefoot. She was running around *barefoot* in the *forest?* That took... tough feet.

"Fine." Girona stuck a couple fingers in her mouth, like one of the stable-boys, and whistled.

A large, well, *picnic basket* came sailing out of the trees behind them. It was floating a few feet off the ground. It halted next to Girona.

Midele had dipped her toes into the stream and winced a little. It was cold, Thony knew that for himself.

"You're still sure you want to do this, Midele?" Girona asked. "That's the boundary with Eyola, you know."

The stream was a boundary with another *world?* Thony looked at it with more interest, comparing the insanely large trees on this side – some of them as wide around as small cottages – with the slightly more normal-sized ones closer to the girls.

"We're just going to have lunch," the taller girl pointed out. "We're not going to go wandering through the Fairy Wood. Not *this* time, anyways," she added, with a tone of concession. "We should definitely prepare a little more if we plan to do *that.*"

She was bunching her skirts up even higher – almost up to her knees – apparently to keep her dress dry as she waded. Thony was uncomfortably aware that *girls* weren't supposed to show their bare legs like this. Even the village girls, whose skirts were only calf-length in the first place, always made sure their stockings covered the gap. *This* girl seemed... as unconcerned about her bare shoulders and legs as her cousin did about her hairstyle and color-choices.

"All right," Girona said nonchalantly, then gave her cousin a bit of a smirk and sailed over the stream between one stride and the next. "Here, baskie, baskie," she cajoled, and the picnic basket sailed over as well.

Midele looked up with a sort of pursed expression and continued to wade through the chilly water without a comment. Thony decided that Proper Princely Behavior required him to offer her a hand up the bank when she approached his side. He decided to ignore the broad hint that Proper Princely Behavior was giving him about stepping into that icy stream to help her across as well. It wasn't like the girl would ever know the difference.

Midele gave him a smile of thanks as she accepted his aid in climbing out of the water.

Girona was already rummaging around in the basket, which continued to hover at about waist-height on her. The red-and-white checked blanket that had covered the other contents had been dumped on the mossy ground. "Spread this out, will you guys?"

Thony and Midele each took an edge and laid out the blanket. He was still feeling rather bemused by this whole encounter, but he was definitely hungry, and surely whatever they had in that basket had to be better than dry cheese and hardtack.

That was definitely true, as Girona began laying out a luncheon to match one of Queen Annabel's nicer teas. A number of small sandwiches, a thermos of – yes – cold sweetened tea, several kinds of small, frosted cakes, and a container that proved to hold cubed pieces of watermelon. There was even a hot sweetmash for Silverfoot. The basket seemed to have more magick to it than its method of transportation, because there was no way that had all fit in the physical volume that Thony could see.

The conversation wasn't bad, either.

A chittery gray mouse that had been hiding in the student wizard's pocket was Girona's pet, Snackers, and a strange scarlet-pink fluffball that didn't seem to have any limbs or eyes and had hidden under Midele's hair was her pet *'nifin'*. Midele also had a couple of other pets that they'd left home, and a rather vast-sounding number of brothers and sisters. Girona had a few siblings as well, but hers were far away. They thought it sounded interesting to be the youngest of three, like Thony, and they were sympathetic about his parents disbanding his circus-act-training program for rats.

And Eyola sounded even weirder than Amanita's 'matriarchal' homeland. Girona and Midele claimed that they didn't have royalty there. Just a lot of people who took turns being in charge or voting for someone to be in charge or something. So, his first impression – that they weren't commoners – wasn't exactly right. But it wasn't exactly *wrong*, either.

The girls were persuaded to trot out that 'compass' they'd kept mentioning. It looked like any other compass, but they claimed it was magickal and that Girona had made it to point to wherever you asked it to go. There were two separate settings, actually: one for the most direct route, and one for the safest route. Midele noted, dryly, that the second one had been *her* idea.

Amanita – and Twinklestar – arrived before they had moved on to the desserts. She was hot and grumpy and out of sorts. There were small twigs stuck in her hair and Twinklestar's mane and tail. And her attitude was *not* improved by coming upon Thony having a very civilized outdoor tea with a pair of strangers... and markedly neither searching for her nor looking particularly concerned.

The introductions and explanations about mirror-selves and so on had to be gone over again, of course. And more sandwiches and little cakes and sweetmash distributed as appropriate.

Amanita permitted herself to be mollified after about her third little cake and several pieces of watermelon.

Twinklestar didn't seem quite as easygoing about the whole thing – although he clearly enjoyed the sweetmash. His ire, however, seemed to be directed at Amanita.

Girona and Amanita got along beautifully, once they got over giving each other suspicious looks and trying to outdo each other in outrageousness. The story of why Thony was running away from home got trotted out in rather more detail than he believed necessary. The reason why *Amanita* had run away from home was somehow glossed over again.

Girona seemed a bit skeptical that Thony's plan could work, but kept most of her opinions about that to herself. She thoroughly approved of the idea of getting out from under parental expectations to go off and do more interesting things. Amanita beamed at her, and Midele looked a bit worried.

"This seems like a rather dangerous way to solve things," she commented.

Thony shrugged. "I don't really have any particularly *good* options right now." He paused. "And I suppose it's less about solving things than buying me some time."

He didn't mention his secondary plan of coming back to his homeworld and sneaking off to his Uncle Louis' kingdom on the sea to look for more amenable princesses with powerful and supportive royal fathers in that region. Fathers with *armies* or at least large numbers of knights that they could lend to make Aldyrwald seem a much less attractive target.

Or vast magickal powers, like his great-great-grandmother's fathers had had.

He also didn't mention that he felt the whole thing was ridiculous. Both of his sisters and one brother-in-law were honest-to-goodness *Deities,* so how could the Devinthals possibly have lost the Divine Right of Kings? If the neighboring royals only *believed* in what had happened, they would all be competing to have their daughters marry Thony and be his future queen, rather than plotting to wed him to an otherwise unmarriageable relative who would then smother him in his sleep or something so that they could add Aldyrwald to their own demesne. And if they *believed,* then none of them would *dare* to consider starting a war to overthrow Papa or rip the mountain-region apart by each trying to snatch up a piece of Aldyrwald themselves.

"I suppose," Midele sighed. "And, who knows. Maybe something *will* change while you're gone."

"Either way, at least he can wait to come back until he's actually a grown up," Girona opined. "Didn't you say that you're old enough to rule on your own at twenty-one?"

More than *six years* to be gone? Thony didn't really want to think about that.

"Old enough to rule doesn't mean old enough to refuse direct orders from your liege-lady – or liege-lord," Amanita told her mirror-self dryly. "That's never actually a thing."

Interesting that *she* understood...

Girona frowned, her noisy little mouse running back and forth across her shoulders. "Then what's the point?"

Thony winced. Put like that, he wasn't actually sure there was one.

"Lots of things can happen in a couple of years," Amanita said, echoing Midele's comment. She stood up and grabbed Girona's shoulder. "Come on. I'm sure there's something else we can talk about besides the sadsack here and his tale of woe. I want to hear all about this wizard stuff. If we're mirror-twins, or whatever, do you think I might be able to do some of it?"

The look the former stable-girl gave Thony was rather more sympathetic than her words had been, but her words served to distract the other girl. Girona also stood up and the two wandered off, talking.

"Girona has... rather strong opinions about things," Midele not-quite apologized, putting the fluffball *nifin* into his hands. It was as soft as it looked. A little weird, if soothing when it started *purring*... given that it didn't seem to have a mouth.

Thony shrugged. “She’s not wrong.”

The novice priestess gave him a wry smile. “No, she usually isn’t. But I’d probably try the same thing you are if I were in your place. And so would she.”

“Hmmn.” Thony didn’t want to dwell on this. He petted the *nifin* absently. “So, tell me about this Goddess of yours. How did you decide to become a priestess?”

Midele’s brown eyes lit up with enthusiasm.

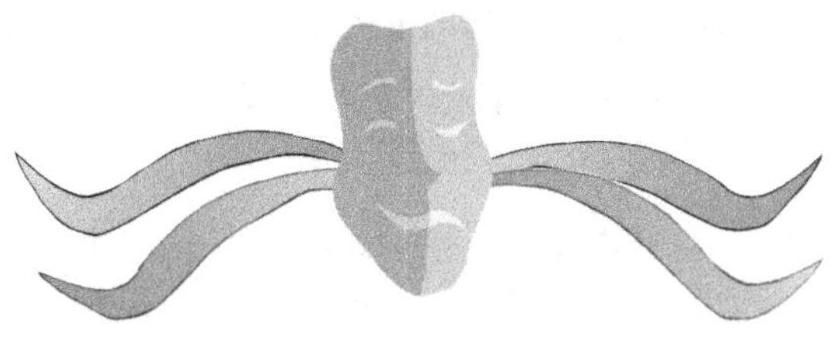

Chapter TWO

Not Carnivorous Plant People

After lunch had stretched on past the point of really being able to call it that, the other girls admitted that they were expected back for dinner by Midele's parents. And since all the trees leading into the Fairy Wood would likely tattle on her if queried – her mother being an honest-to-goodness *dryad* – they couldn't stay too terribly much longer.

The young priestess-to-be got a determined look on her face as they packed up the lunch things, and dragged her cousin off a ways to talk or argue or something. Snackers, the mouse, definitely seemed to be arguing anyways. Finally, Girona threw up her hands – literally – and came stumping back over to Thony and Amanita.

"Midele has a bee up her butt about the two of you getting lost. We know our way back home, so we don't really need the compass any more. But I only set it up to work for *us,* so I need to modify it a bit. Amanita, you wanted to see if you could do magick, right? Let's give it a go."

She plopped herself down on the now-empty picnic blanket and pulled out the small device. Amanita knelt down next to her with a look of fascination.

Midele drew Thony away from the pair, taking her scarlet fluffball pet back from him as she did so. "Girona hates to have me looking over her shoulder. She thinks I criticize too much."

That seemed a bit backwards to Thony, but he'd known the pair of them for all of a couple hours, so what did he know. Still, it never hurt to practice Gallantry, according to Roger.

"I'm sure that isn't true."

The girl grinned. "Well, *I* would say it isn't, of course. Come here. I can't do what Girona does with magick, but I have an idea of my own."

She led the way to an oak tree of particularly impressive girth, put the *nifin* on her shoulder, tucked under a lock of her long, wavy, auburn hair, and laid a hand on the trunk just below the first major branch. The spot she chose was just below shoulder-height on Thony.

"I can't *guide* you somewhere else, but I think I can make us all a *beacon* to let us find this place again," she said, her brow furrowed with concentration. "If she'll let me."

"She?" Thony asked.

"The oak."

Oh. He wasn't used to people who talked to trees.

"She says 'yes'," Midele said after a moment of what might have been negotiations. "You need to put your hand on this same spot for a moment – no, I mean *after* I move my hand away..."

Thony had stepped up behind her and covered her hand with his slightly larger one. He flushed for some reason as she looked over her shoulder at him.

"Sorry..."

"No problem." As soon as he had stepped back, she moved her hand aside and gestured him back to try again. "I'm going to have Girona and Amanita do the same thing. They're mirror-selves, of course, so they can probably find each other without this sort of help, especially now that they know each other. But this way they can find *us* as well, or we can find this place again. I haven't done this before, but if I did it right, the oak should let all of us within her range know if one of us comes back here."

She was babbling a little, Thony thought. Well, she'd never done this spell – or whatever – before, so she was probably nervous about whether it would work.

A moment later she had the other girls pressing their palms to the same spot.

"It's not much, I know," Midele half-apologized. "But it's possible to lose the compass. And this oak will always be here. We'll all be able to locate this spot, no matter where we end up in the Fairy Wood, at least... and since Eyola is right there," she gestured past the stream, "it's an easy way to find a safe place."

"How will we know where this tree is?" Amanita asked in an interested way.

Midele looked embarrassed. "I'm not really sure. My mother has done this for each of us, but I haven't had to test it. And I don't think any of my brothers or sisters has either." She had a number of each, she'd admitted, with several older and younger both. A *middle child,* Thony had categorized her somewhat dismissively – on his world, middleborn princes and princesses weren't significant. Except for Roger, of course. And

Priscilla. Not that Midele – and even her *name* was middling – was royalty. It didn't really matter for anyone else, except maybe for worthy miller's daughters, and she wasn't one of those either. "Actually... I'm less sure about whether the tree will act as a *beacon* or whether it will only send a message to the rest of us if one of us gets here. You'll have to touch that exact spot as well," she added.

Girona rolled her eyes and Snackers chittered his own lack of enthusiasm. "Well, the compass should be more useful. You can set it on *anything* you want and it should guide you there."

"Hmmn." Midele looked at her. "Give it to me a minute. Did you add the third setting like I asked you to?"

"Yeah." Girona handed over the small disk. "What is that for, anyways? You said leave it for you to give it a meaning. That wasn't *easy,*" she added pointedly. "The basic spell wasn't hard, but turning it into an FPGA was a challenge. A Focused-Potential Geas Acceptor," she 'clarified' condescendingly to the uncomprehending expressions of the rest.

The taller girl's long, dark hair fell forward to hide her face as she bent over the compass. She wasn't really *tall,* Thony thought absently, just taller than Amanita and Girona. And she was fifteen, slightly older than him, whereas the other girls were barely past fourteen.

"There," Midele said with relief. "I think it worked. It's... a priestess-thing, I guess. I prayed to the Golden Sphinx to fix that final setting to point the way to what you *truly seek,* even if you aren't sure what it is." She gave the compass to Thony, and then gave Amanita a wry look. "Given the kind of quests you're both on, I figured that might come in handy at some point."

Wait a moment. What did she mean by the quests they were *both* on?

Amanita looked somewhat impressed and spoke before Thony could ask the question. "Heart-magick. That's not simple stuff where I come from."

Midele smiled shyly at her, then glanced at her cousin. "Not that it would have been at all useful if Girona hadn't created this awesome compass in the first place." That seemed a little over-the-top, if not for the wry grin she gave her cousin. Their close friendship was easy to see now, and the way they teased each other was mostly comfortable to be around.

The colorfully dressed student wizard preened a little in appreciation of the compliment, but looked thoughtful. "I wish you'd told me what you planned, Midele. Maybe I could have made that setting separate – like a toggle switch for what you *want* and what you *need*. That way they could have used either the *direct* or *safe-path* options with it. As it is, it's only going to point directly."

Midele winced and looked worried. "I didn't think of that."

Thony gave her a reassuring smile. "It's far more than we could have imagined having."

"Besides which, we can surely use our own common-sense to avoid problematic situations," Amanita put in, "and then reorient on our goal with the compass."

She narrowed her eyes as Midele and Thony both looked at the younger girls with a certain skepticism, but Girona laughed and clapped her mirror-self on the shoulder. "Sometimes the best things are the ones you find because you *didn't* do the prudent thing."

Her cousin nodded a little wryly, and with a certain relief. "The Golden Sphinx works through serendipity."

"You've been awfully kind," Thony commented. "And we haven't given you anything back."

Girona shrugged. “So, pay it forward and help someone else when you have the chance. Or else come back here and we’ll make things even then. Midele and I are planning on going adventuring someday; we kind of hope there will be people who help *us* for no particular reward, so it makes sense to start the karmic cycle.”

Her words seemed to hit Amanita particularly hard for some reason, because the former stable-girl’s eyes went wide and surprised, though she didn’t say anything.

Midele nodded, then hesitated. “There’s... another reason, too...”

“I told Amanita,” Girona nudged her cousin. “And we need to start getting back before Uncle Herush decides to have Aunt Linden start quizzing the trees on our whereabouts.”

The older girl sighed. “All right. Take care, you guys. I hope we’ll see you again.”

“Come visit us in Eyola,” Girona added, and this time she floated *both* of them across the stream in addition to the picnic basket.

They waved goodbye and vanished into the trees on the other side of the stream, bickering amiably as the picnic basket floated after them. Midele turned back to wave, just before they disappeared into the trees.

Thony shook his head in bemusement, dropping the hand he’d raised in a belated farewell. The whole thing seemed unreal, now that the odd pair were out of sight, but the small, thick disk of the compass was still in his other hand.

“Well,” Amanita said after a moment, “*that* was weird.”

“Yeah...” Thony looked at his friend. “Weirder for you, I suppose. What was the other reason they were helping us?”

Amanita winced. “Apparently there’s a wizardly theory that if *one* mirror-self dies, so do all the others.”

Thony choked a little. "I'm almost surprised they didn't give us even *more* help, then."

The former stable-girl shrugged. "There's that karmic-debt cycle she mentioned, too, though. The more you give away, the more will come back to you... and the more you take, the more you end up having to give up. *Another* theory suggests that the debt incurred by *one* mirror-self is owed by all of them. And there's some question about whether a transfer from one analogue to another counts as a debt or not. Or whether that sort of thing seriously messes with a bunch of other stuff and causes other problems to befall at least the pair that made the exchange. Which is why she gave the compass to Midele, and Midele gave it to *you.*"

"Hunh." Thony looked at the compass more thoughtfully. "Well, we're off the path that you were familiar with. Do you think we should use it *now* to get to your homeworld?"

"There's a thought." Amanita sounded hesitant. "It's also mid-afternoon, and we're not exactly in a rush and this is a nice spot. We could just make camp here and go on in the morning."

Thony tilted his head at her. "There's something you're not telling me."

Amanita glowered at him. "Quite a number of things actually."

"I've noticed," Thony said dryly. "Nothing that has to do with our safety, I'm sure. I *do* trust you, you know."

She sagged a little in relief. "Yeah. I do. You were following me without arguing or complaining any earlier when I was being a..." She winced.

"A grouch," he filled in when she hesitated. "It's okay," Thony added magnanimously. "You came out to make sure I didn't get into trouble in the Fairy Wood without me warning you I was leaving or anything. And I know you weren't planning to go home yet. Though I don't know *why,*" he noted a little pointedly.

"And it wasn't either of our faults that there... was something dangerous enough to spook Silverfoot," Amanita ignored his broad hint as adeptly as ever. "Even Twinkie was pretty freaked out when we saw the *findilaar.*"

Twinklestar snorted derisively and turned himself around so his rear end was facing the girl.

Amanita winced. "Okay. Twinklestar was *concerned* because he had to look out for such vulnerable creatures as the other three of us. *Findilaar* are pretty freaky to look at, with those bat-wings and all those eyes and the teeth, but not too hard to avoid if you know what you're doing."

The unicorn looked back at them over his shoulder and gave a small, regal nod. Thony was struck once again by the subtle differences between Twinklestar and a pony. The unicorn's eyes were slightly more forwards-facing, for example, so that he had less peripheral vision than an equine – or than the overgrown goat he also vaguely resembled. He could look at you and meet your eyes much better than a horse and his eyes were more... human-shaped as well. And then the spiraling horn that looked like star-brushed ivory – a rather useless description, but it was what came to the young prince's mind. His coat was white – but, again, it seemed to *glimmer* somehow, when shadows crossed it, for all that it looked pretty normal in regular daylight or even torchlight.

Twinklestar was looking back at Thony with... could that be a *speculative* look?

"Yeah, let's make camp here," Thony agreed, tearing his gaze away and scanning the glade, for all that he'd looked at every bit of it already. "Should we go across the stream? Those girls said their world was safe."

Amanita tilted her head to the side. "I'm not sure if that's exactly what they said. I think it was that there would be safe places we could *get to* if we crossed the stream. Like Midele's home, presumably. It can't be far away if they were able to come out here as a day excursion. Her parents sound nearly as over-protective as mi– yours. According to Girona."

"Hmmn." Thony hadn't missed her quick self-correction. "So long as whatever it was that freaked out *Silverfoot* doesn't find us here. A *'findilaar'* you called it?"

Twinklestar had turned himself around and shook his head in a very equine movement that somehow suggested no such creature would *dare* bother them while *he* was on watch.

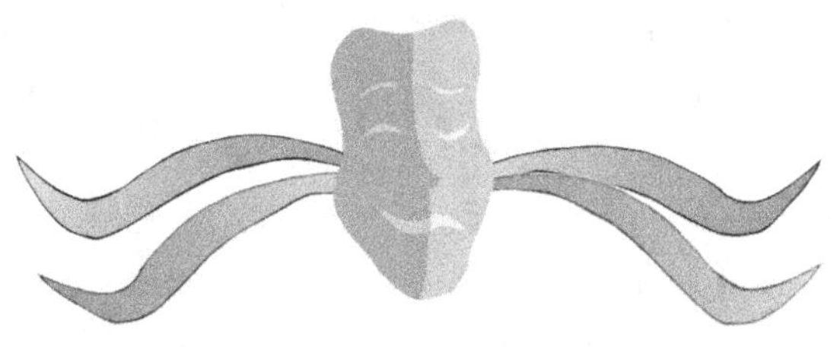

Chapter THREE

Unicorn-Maiden *Issues*

THE SLIGHT CHILL THAT HAD fallen when the sun set and shadows filled the Fairy Wood kept Thony awake for awhile, but seemed to abate after he fell asleep. At least he *felt* warm and safe. And dry.

It was obvious *why* he had slept so well when he woke up.

Twinklestar had laid down carefully next to him at some point. Apparently, the unicorn didn't particularly appreciate dew either and had done something about it that had benefited Thony as well.

From the other side of their banked fire, Amanita looked much less comfy. And annoyed.

It made for a bad start to what surely was going to be a long day.

Nothing was helped when Twinklestar refused to let Amanita saddle and bridle him, let alone load him up with her packs.

"Twinklestar, *dammit!*" the feisty girl exclaimed at last, dropping her saddle on the ground and stamping her foot in more frustration than Thony had ever seen her express after the umpteenth time the unicorn curvetted away from her attempts. "If you don't want to be ridden anymore, *fine*. I can ride double with Thony. Or walk. But I need to transport all this *stuff*. We can put my packs on Silverfoot, but he can't carry a second saddle."

Twinklestar stuck his nose in the air and pranced a few steps farther away, clearly unconcerned with these human problems.

Amanita bit her lip, and looked at Thony worriedly. "Saddles are... expensive. I don't want to just leave it here. But it seems kind of stupid to try to call Girona back just to ask her to keep the saddle for us. I don't even know when – or if – we'll be back."

Not to mention that if Twinklestar changed his mind about letting her ride, she'd be stuck with the unicorn's bony spine under her butt. That didn't sound comfortable for either of them.

"And how she'd carry it anywhere..." Thony remembered the floating picnic basket. "Well, I guess that's not actually a problem, with her magick." He was sort of curious about visiting Eyola – a world where magick was used as trivially and ubiquitously as both girls had implied sounded... interesting.

Should he suggest they do that – visit Eyola – instead of going on to... whatever Amanita's homeworld was called. Another thing she'd never mentioned. Not that it had occurred to him that *worlds* would have *names* to distinguish them, just like countries did, before they'd met the other girls. Apparently, it hadn't really sunk into his thick skull that there were *lots* of worlds out here...

He sighed a little at his own stupidity and reached up to rub the velvety nose that was nudging his shoulder, but he managed not to say what he was thinking. Amanita would be too likely to agree.

"Well, if that doesn't beat all." Now the girl sounded irritated rather than concerned. Again.

"What now?" Thony asked with a less discreet sigh, as his scratching fingers moved to one of Silverfoot's favorite itchy spots on the crown of his brow and encountered...

"Oh," Thony said in realization.

Amanita was giving both him and the unicorn a dirty look.

"Fine," she said before Thony had quite figured out what to say. She went over to Silverfoot, already dressed and ready to go and demurely nibbling on a nearby bush, and began shortening his stirrups. "I suppose we can switch out saddlebags in the morning."

"Um, what?" Thony was fairly sure he knew what she was saying, but...

Twinklestar nudged him again, and he jumped a little as he felt horse drool dampening his shoulder and something dangling down along with it... He jumped *carefully* because, well, that *horn*...

The unicorn had the bridle in his mouth – not properly, but all scrunched up as if he'd just picked it up off the ground. And he was clearly offering it to Thony.

The young prince gave the magickal equine a somewhat sickly smile, but took the offering and fitted the bridle carefully over Twinklestar's head, trying to ignore the drying greenish slime on his shoulder. The unicorn was at least a hand *shorter* than the old pony that Thony had outgrown. If he used the stirrups at the length Amanita had kept them, his knees would be poking up higher than his bellybutton. And if he lengthened them, they'd be dragging on the ground.

But when a creature of great and unknown magickal power offered you a gift like this... well, it wasn't really *wise* or... *Proper Princely Behavior* to refuse. He had some sense of how Priscilla must have felt all these months with Twinklestar furious because she had been supposed to be *his* unicorn-maiden and instead she was a Goddess and *married*.

No, Twinklestar let him know, he had no idea. And would he please just get on with this. They had places to go and people to see.

Who? Thony wanted to know, but the idea that *something* interesting was going to happen sped up his work and the saddle and packs went on quickly.

He cast a half-regretful, half-relieved look at his weapons, still attached to Silverfoot's saddle, as he mounted. There was no way he could possibly attach them to the much smaller saddle Twinklestar was wearing. But on the other hand, that reduced the temptation to try to *use* them... which was probably a good thing, considering he'd never used a sword of edged steel at all and his aim with the bow and arrows was pretty chancy.

Twinklestar informed him that he had seen Thony at practice with Roger and Jeremy and the young prince was *terrible* with archery and shouldn't be allowed near a blade of any kind. But there was no reason to fear, because he, Twinklestar would make it all work out.

Lovely, Thony thought as he posted along on the unicorn's back – one thing made easier by these awkward stirrups at least. He tried not even to *think* about how they'd already strayed off the path once because of some mysterious monstrous beast and Twinklestar had done nothing about *that* at all...

Strayed, but not come to harm, Twinklestar assured him loftily, adding a little extra pop into his trot as a punishment for such skepticism. And they'd met those girls, and that had been something Important. Just like what they were headed towards next.

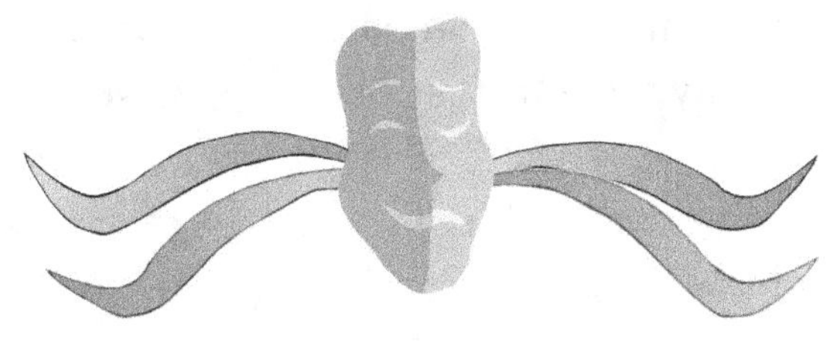

Chapter FOUR

More Unicorn-Maiden Issues

'NEXT' WAS APPARENTLY A LOOSE concept for unicorns, Thony thought sourly as they made their third camp in the Fairy Wood.

The awkward riding position had made him almost too stiff to move when they came to a halt yesterday morning. And Twinklestar's gait had never yet improved, so likely this was just something Thony was going to have to get used to. At least the sharp, hot soreness was beginning to fade into a dull ache that made him totter around like an old man.

A day or two more and maybe he'd be almost back to normal.

He cast a resentful look at the blithe Amanita, who looked perfectly fine after two days on the smooth-gaited Silverfoot. First, she took over his *Quest,* then his *horse...*

"Do you think you can either curry the equines or make dinner tonight?" she asked in an almost too-nice tone, and Thony eyed her suspiciously.

She'd gone from grumpy about, well *everything* to almost overly solicitous by the time they had stopped yesterday. Which had been just as well, since he'd been unable to move without excruciating pain, and she'd had to do all the work of setting up camp. And the same this morning.

She'd even made him a special tea that she said would help. Something from the mountains where she grew up that she'd been saving for emergencies. *'Arnica'*, she called it, and she had him put cloths soaked in it on his sore body parts, rather than drink it – which was what *he* had always thought one did with tea. It was a little awkward to do this, but he suspected that, indeed, he wasn't in anywhere near as much pain as he deserved after riding in that cramped position for two days. So...

"I think that 'tea' is helping," Thony said grudgingly. "I'd... rather curry the equines, I suppose."

That could *mostly* be done standing, though Silverfoot was developing an annoying habit of sidestepping. Cooking would require collecting wood, fetching water, building a fire – and Amanita had built the fires so far – and then actually turning the dried stores of food into something edible. Not only did that involve a great deal more bending and straightening, but Thony was still fairly uncertain about the process of cooking. Oh, he understood it in *concept* and *he'd* be willing to choke down whatever mess he created while he made his first forays into the field... but he wasn't sure his pickier friend would put up with him 'ruining' dinner.

Amanita just nodded affably, and reminded him to be sure to check the hooves.

An hour or so later, Thony eased himself, wincingly, onto his poor abused buttocks to accept a bowl of whatever Amanita had prepared. Stew of some kind. Nutritious and... pretty damn good, actually. Maybe it didn't rival the creations of her nemesis in the Royal Kitchens of Aldyrwald, but Thony had never been so hungry when he was at home either, and the old saw about hunger being the best spice was utterly true.

He shot Twinklestar a sharp look while savoring another bite of stew. That wasn't a saying from *Aldyrwald.*

The unicorn ignored him and went on blissfully enjoying the hot mash Amanita had thoughtfully put together for him and Silverfoot.

"Are we going to have enough food for this trip?" Thony asked, now looking at the bowls the two equines were eating out of. "If we're cooking food for them also? I had assumed Silverfoot would mostly be grazing."

Amanita shrugged without a great deal of concern. "We're not going to be in the Fairy Wood for long. We can buy stuff once we get to farms and towns and all."

Thony frowned at that. "I... don't really have all *that* much money with me." He winced. "Not that I have any idea how much things will cost on your world."

She gave him a slightly exasperated look. "You keep saying that as if it's all one piece. Does everything cost the same in Aldyrwald as in, oh, Schwannsberg? Or – what was the name of that kingdom you keep going on about where your uncle married the mermaid?"

"Perldelmar," Thony answered automatically. He had *not* 'gone on' about Uncle Louis that he could recall. "No. I suppose not. Though I've never been there, so I couldn't really say for sure. The things we send for from the coast are pretty dear..."

Her complaint was reasonably valid.

"Okay," he said, setting the bowl down to try to adjust his posture into putting pressure on a different bruise. "So... where will we be coming out of the Fairy Wood? And how much do things cost *there?*"

Amanita ladled another dollop of stew into his mostly-empty bowl. He'd complained the first night that she ate between a third and a fourth of what she prepared and insisted he eat the rest. He'd complained, not because he wasn't hungry enough to eat it all, but because it didn't seem gentlemanly to scarf it all down like a ravening beast while she sat there and daintily picked at her own serving. The girl had merely raised an eyebrow at him – he'd been scraping his bowl for traces of gravy for the third time – and informed him that she'd make sure she got enough to eat, not to worry. And oh, by the way, he could scrape down the pot if he liked.

He still remembered her sharp words about him being fat when they'd first met...

...but she'd seemed sincere enough...

... and there had been several spoons-worth in the pot.

The next day she'd increased the total amount.

Right now, Amanita was looking at him with something that might almost be mistaken for approval in a... hmmn... *lesser* person.

"If things go according to my plan, we'll come out by Quellarie's cottage," she informed him. "She's... sort of an expert in the Fairy Wood. As much as anyone can be that is, besides the elves and fairies."

"Quellarie Unicorn-Born?" Thony found himself asking, though he had no idea why that term or title or whatever-it-was had popped into his mind.

Amanita gave him an odd look. "Yes. That's who I mean. How do you...?" Her eyes widened as her gaze went over Thony's shoulder. "Oh! He's talking to you. *He's* talking to *you.*"

Disappointment colored the last bit.

Twinklestar made a *whuffling* noise practically in Thony's ear and he jumped.

"Don't you *dare* drool on me again," he informed the unicorn. "Grass makes *stains,* and I haven't even had a chance to wash out the last bunch of goo. How am I supposed to stay presentable enough to win a princess if my shoulders are covered with green stains? And if you want to tell her it would never have worked out between you, you can do it *yourself.*"

It was a unicorn-maiden's job to translate for the unicorn, Twinklestar informed him loftily and then made his point about who was in charge of whom by drooling on Thony. In his hair, though, not on his shirt.

Not really an improvement.

At all.

Though presumably his hair wouldn't stain.

Amanita was looking... utterly bemused as Thony swore rather benignly. But he'd noticed that her vocabulary of expletives wasn't any more extensive than his own all the way back in Aldyrwald and had no compunctions.

"Are you saying he says you're his *unicorn-maiden?*" she asked after a few minutes of his not-so-sulfurous oaths not so much as warming the air, let alone blistering it like in stories. They were camped for the night in a nice little glade, but the spring that she'd collected water from was barely a trickle and nowhere near enough to do much about his hair. The perpetrator of the damage was regarding him with not so hidden amusement. "Well. Well, well, *well,* well, well."

Thony stopped trying to finger-comb the goo out and wipe it on the ground, and glared at her. "Yeah, that's what he said. Wanna make something of it?"

She rolled her eyes. "Puh-*lease.* The term is generic for both boys and girls. At least where I come from it is, and I think

Twinklestar may be from my world?" She tilted her head at the unicorn in a gesture of question.

Twinklestar nodded his head, then shook it. And looked significantly at Thony.

Who averted his eyes and muttered some more useless and mild cursewords.

It didn't really help that Amanita's snickers sounded more like they were about her not crying than actually laughing at him. Thony glared back at her, and the snickers became a smirk.

"Thony's a *unicorn-maiden,* hoo-boy! If only Wes could hear *this!*"

The result of that comment was a mad dash, zigzagging around their campsite that ended with Amanita in a tree rather higher than he could reach, singing out "Nyah-nyah-nyuh-nyahh-nyah... You can't catch me!"

Well, he probably *could,* if his muscles weren't still so... wait a minute. All that running around had actually stretched out his sore rear-end and things more than he'd been willing to force himself to do without the, ah, *encouragement.* Thony looked at the smooth-skinned tree she'd shinnied up so easily with some speculation. It resembled the beech trees at home, but had different leaves; no branches for the first six or seven feet, and that was the one she was sitting on. He wasn't any good at shinnying *(to his own disgust, but after trying for literally* **years** *one had to accept one's limitations)* but he had grown enough that maybe he could *jump* and grab that branch and haul himself up...

"Nevermind," the girl said hastily as he gathered himself for a straight-jump. She slithered off the branch and dropped practically on top of him.

"Caught you," Thony said without much satisfaction from the ground. She'd all but gotten her foot in his eye, and knocked them both down. And she definitely deserved frogs in her bedroll.

Well, except for the really great food she'd been making.

Darn it. Revenge or good food? Making adult decisions was *hard*.

"Well, this is going to be a bit of a mess," Amanita said as they headed back to their campfire. They hadn't gone very far, given the risk of ending up in Very Wrong Places. "I don't think I've ever heard of a *guy* being a unicorn-maiden before."

Thony narrowed his eyes at her. "I am *not* a unicorn-maiden."

She shrugged. "Whatever, dude. If Twinkie's going to insist on you riding him after we exit the Wood, we'll have to find *some* sort of explanation as to why you're riding the pudgy pony and I'm on the big fancy horse."

Thony grunted, while Twinklestar looked offended. "I thought you said *girls* were in charge of everything over there."

Amanita winced a little. "No. Not mostly. That's at home. Though most of the places I've been don't particularly *care* about whether someone is a boy or girl... there's still certain... let's say *expectations* about boys and girls. Or men and women. That are the opposite of what we have in Path– I mean at home. Where things are done more sensibly."

She'd almost named her homeland there, he rather thought. 'Paahth-something' it had sounded like. And 'expectations' sounded like maybe her descriptions of egalitarianism were a bit overblown outside of her own homeland.

"'Expectations'?" Thony quoted her. "Like what?"

The girl shrugged irritably, though he almost thought she looked relieved that he wasn't asking about her home. "You know. Having guys do the heavy lifting and more of the fighting.

Not that there aren't a *huge* number of famous mercenaries and knights and such who are women!" she added quickly and defensively.

Famous because they were rare? Stories tended to circulate about unusual occurrences, Thony knew, and they stayed alive to keep being passed around if they were unusual *enough*. Like Prissy's tail.

Probably not worth arguing about, though. He'd see for himself soon enough.

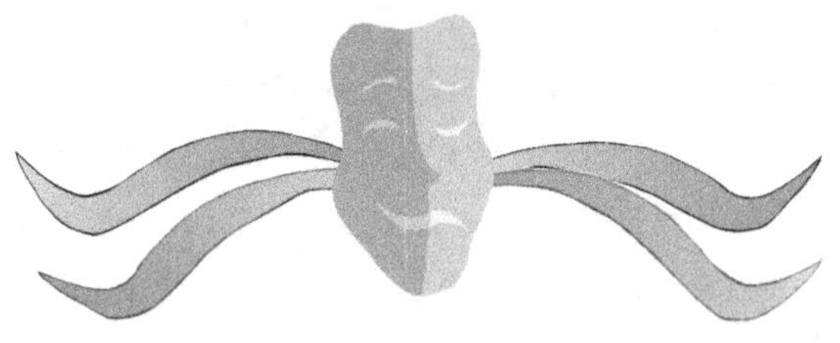

Chapter FIVE

Reasons to Run Away

THE NEXT MORNING, AMANITA DECIDED it was time for him to learn how to make breakfast.

They ended up eating more of the dry cheese and hard-tack – which they were able to find once all the smoke blew away. Thony felt it was entirely unfair of her to be irritated with him for ruining breakfast when it was all her fault that he hadn't known the frying pan was too hot for bacon.

They had bigger problems to worry about, however, since the compass that Girona and Midele had given them – and that they had been using to point their way to the safest way out of the Fairy Wood decided to go haywire.

"It's doing *what?*" Amanita demanded when he and Twinklestar came to a smooth halt.

Now that Thony had admitted he could communicate – somehow – with the unicorn, the ride had become easier, since Twinklestar responded to his non-verbal requests and warned him about bumps and things the same way. It still wasn't exactly *comfortable,* but then Twinklestar wasn't trained as a saddle-beast. Thony tried not to think too hard the hope that the unicorn would pick up some tricks from Silverfoot – for both their sakes, since he'd taken over the tasks Amanita had been doing while he was too sore and was now treating Twinklestar's aches and raw-spots from his own unexpected exercise.

Suggesting that Amanita would be a lighter load had gotten him a disdainful sniff and some more green drool into his caked hair.

"It keeps switching around," Thony repeated what he had just said. He was staring at the small disk in perplexity. "Or, no... maybe it's pointing to something that's moving. Circling us?"

He looked up and apprehensively at the trees that had dark shadows between them only a dozen yards in any given direction.

"You sure you have it set on *safest* route to where we want to *go?*" Amanita demanded. "I can think of a half-dozen things that might get us out *more directly* – including getting eaten by a *glypherthryp* that lives just outside and forages here. Or another *findilaar* chasing us into another world."

Thony gave her a distracted look. "A what? A who?"

The girl rolled her eyes. "I told you about the *findilaar.* The bat-winged thing with four eyes that was what spooked Silverfoot into running off back at the beginning."

The young prince shuddered delicately. She'd gone into rather more detail than he'd really wanted when she'd described the thing previously. He was an imaginative young man and... he hadn't really needed that much detail. Twinklestar let him know that he didn't have to worry about *findilaar;* all one needed to do was head off through thick brush and out of such a creature's flight-path, since they didn't maneuver terribly well, then circle back around. Which Silverfoot had done by instinct, except for the circling around part.

Thony ignored this.

"And the other one?"

Now it was *Amanita* who shuddered. "You don't want to know more about glypherthryp."

Since he'd decided he hadn't really wanted to know about the *findilaar,* he decided to let that one lie.

"It's set on *safest,*" he held it out for her to see. "And the thing Midele added isn't on. So, it should be pointing to where we want to go, shouldn't it?"

Amanita peered down from her greater height on Silverfoot. "Yeah, that's what I would've thought, anyways." She watched the little arrow continue its slow migration. "It sure does look like something is circling us. And that *something* must be the key to our safest way out of the Fairy Wood. Or... where did you tell it you wanted it to take us?"

"You said to tell it to take you home until we got out of the Wood," Thony reminded her. "So that we'd end up on the right world."

"Oh, yeah." The girl shook her head. "I kind of assumed it would take us back the way I came in the first place, through the Perushin village. And end us up at Quellarie's cottage. But neither of those should be *moving around.*"

"So whad'you think it means?" Thony asked, perplexed.

The girl shrugged. "I dunno. Maybe we should just stay here and see what happens."

"That's a terrible idea. What if it is something dangerous?"

"Can't be," Amanita pointed out. "It's supposed to be our *safest way* to go."

Thony pursed his lips. "What if it's some sort of *key* to our safest way, but there's something dangerous chasing *it,* and *that's* why it's moving around?" The little arrow had moved almost halfway around the circle now, and it was still going.

Amanita gave him a look of almost-respect. "That's not a half-bad explanation. But I don't see what we can do about it. If *we* try to follow where that arrow is pointing and – whatever it is – *is* being chased, then we're likely to run into whatever is chasing it anyways."

Which made altogether too much sense.

"We could set up some sort of prank," Thony suggested. "To stop it or trap it or distract it, depending on what it turns out to be."

Amanita rolled her eyes. "A prank. On the fly. With no planning and next to no resources."

"Your frog pranks in the castle didn't exactly reek of deeply-laid planning," he told her dryly. "Nor were they particularly extravagant in the use of materials."

"And look how poorly they went," she replied without even wincing. "We did much better when we collected that week's worth of spoiled eggs and left them as a minefield for... oh, wait, you didn't know about that... did you..."

Thony gave her a narrowed look. "You decided to muck about with the *Royal Kitchens?* I thought the three of us decided that setting it up so that David and Paul had to work together would be enough, since they hate each other."

"That was all you and Wes," she said breezily. "*I* thought it would take too long. And besides, they'd be miserable, but they wouldn't know *I* had anything to do with it. So, I got the eggs and Wes and I set them up an hour or so before I found out you were running off."

"Where did you put them?" Thony asked, with a certain trepidation.

"Oh, in their rooms," Amanita replied. "We set it up so that the eggs would roll out from under their beds when they shifted around while sleeping."

The young prince let go of the useless reins and rubbed his freed hand over his face. It must have stunk to high-heaven... but you had to admire the engineering that must have gone into that... assuming it worked the way she said it was supposed to. "How do you know the eggs weren't just going to roll out before they went to bed?"

"We tested it, of course," Amanita said loftily.

"Of course... and how are they supposed to know it was you? Were you planning to be there in the morning to tell them or something?"

She looked slightly offended. "And smell that stink? No, I had letters posted to them both."

"'Ha-ha, from Amanita'?" Thony asked.

"Something like that," she agreed. "Though I signed it 'vengeance is served'. I didn't use any of our names."

"Oh. Good." Thony shook his head. This girl had a rather... too enthusiastic taste for revenge. On the other hand, he *had* pranked the entire royalty for three kingdoms out when he was six because they'd been mean to Priscilla. So, he had some sympathy.

On the other hand, *he* had learned better.

When he was *six*.

"It probably helped mask our departure," Amanita pointed out.

"Um."

Because *Mama* was likely to be distracted from the disappearance of her youngest child because a couple of the cooks were smelly. Not.

It probably *had* left the kitchens in an uproar, though, since David was the son of the Chief Cook and Paul was the senior assistant pastry chef. *Someone* had probably been in a rage to identify the prankster, and... oh.

He looked at Amanita in mingled resentment and awe.

"You're thinking it probably all got pinned on *me,* and Mama would have assumed that I was in hiding because it all went too far."

Oh, dear Go– his Sisters. He really *couldn't* go home again for awhile, even if this adventure turned out to be a problem. If the Chief Cook had resigned over this, Mama would just about *kill* him.

"Oh, look, the arrow's stopped moving," Amanita commented interestedly.

It had. The pointer had made a complete circumambulation of the periphery of the disk and was now pointing... straight ahead.

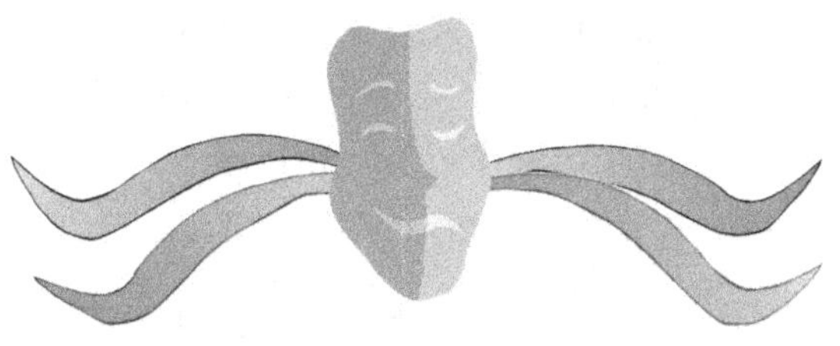

Chapter SIX

You Shall Be Queen

THONY RUBBED AT HIS ACHING head. First these unexpected revelations and now a persistent ringing in his ears while he and Amanita and Twinklestar pensively watched the trees ahead of them.

Well, he and Amanita were pensive. The unicorn had decided to have a snack and was grazing just like Silverfoot. The horse wasn't bright enough to understand, but Twinklestar had no excuses.

"Maybe we should go meet – whatever it is," Thony suggested, trying to keep his fraying temper together. They'd both dismounted, not wanting to risk a repeat of the *findilaar*-incident, and the girl was bouncing on her toes in anticipation while Thony stewed over her revelations about what was likely going on at home.

He'd learned years ago about how far a prank could go before it wasn't appreciated by anyone else. And that revenge pranks brought more trouble than they were worth. He'd been on-board with the idea of getting Amanita's two nemeses to have to deal with each other – it had seemed like they'd both learn a lesson about respecting boundaries and other people if they had to do that, given who they both were.

David had an attitude that everything in the kitchen was his to mess around with – and although he usually shared out the largesse of his excursions into the treats-cabinet with the other castle children, including Thony, there was always a sense that it was a Big Favor and at some point, you'd have to Pay Him Back. He'd gotten a little 'handsy' with Amanita when she was working there as a scullery-girl, and while he hadn't taken it *too* far when she made it clear she wasn't interested, she'd thought it was likely he'd try again. And Thony hadn't been able to disagree with that assessment, even though this was new territory for David, who was about the same age as the young prince.

Paul, on the other hand, had gotten Amanita demoted to scullery-girl from apprentice pastry-chef by using her tools without asking until she'd gotten fed up. She'd switched her own sugar and salt containers – which wouldn't have been a problem for Paul, if he hadn't grabbed hers – and then he'd sabotaged the dessert she'd been asked to make to replace the one he'd ruined.

The pair of them deserved each other, and Thony had been quietly planting the idea that David – whose father seemed to think he was a genius and who honestly *was* likely to inherit his father's position eventually – should learn about the pastry-side of the kitchen operations. Mama – Queen Annabel – had been receptive to the notion, and Thony had expected to see some reorganizations happening within the next few days.

If Mama happened to remember that it had been *Thony* who suggested putting the two cooks together who both ended up smelling like rotten eggs as the result of a very obvious prank – complete with obnoxious letters not-exactly claiming credit... Well, it wouldn't have looked good for him when he wasn't around to deny it.

If anyone would even believe him after the relatively recent rat-circus fiasco even if he *had* been around to deny it.

Not that his rat-training program had *hurt* anyone.

Even if Mama *had* fainted a number of times.

"I think we're good waiting here," Amanita said complacently.

Okay, maybe it was just *Thony* watching the trees with anxiety that had as much to do with stewing about the situation he'd left at home as it did with concern over whatever was about to emerge.

"Did you prank people like this at home?" Thony asked her.

The girl shrugged. "Some. If they deserved it."

"No wonder *you* had to run away from home," Thony muttered, rubbing his aching head again.

She raised her eyebrows and looked down her nose at him. Her nose was a great deal straighter than his, even if she was a great deal shorter, so it was unpleasantly effective. "That was uncalled for, *Your Highness.*"

Well... and she wasn't wrong. That had been a rude thing to say. Even if it probably was true.

"My head hurts," Thony said in a semi-apologetic tone. "It's hard to think. I don't know what happened, but there's this annoying ringing in my ears – *now* what?"

Amanita had started giggling. "That's a real ringing, Thony. Those are fairy-bells."

That... explained absolutely nothing.

"Meaning what?" Maybe he should have gone off to that disturbingly egalitarian-sounding Eyola with Midele and Girona. There might not be any princesses there, but it could hardly have been any worse than trying to travel with a vengeance-obsessed stable-girl and a unicorn who wanted him to be a unicorn-maiden.

"Meaning–" Amanita was distracted before she even really started to explain.

Thony gritted his teeth in his aching head – which just made it worse, but what else could he do? – and reminded himself that Girona Starshine had seemed at least as annoying as his current companion. And since she had magick – and, Amanita had told him later, was sort of *dedicated* to the Eyolan God of Mischief in addition to the Eyolan Goddess of Sorcery – she'd probably have ended up turning *him* into a frog and using him for a prank as soon as the two of them ended up in a real argument. At least Amanita didn't have any magickal powers like that.

That he knew of.

Though if she did, and with her temper, surely he'd have noticed.

The other girl, Midele, had seemed pretty even-tempered. And even like she had a sense of humor. Though she hadn't said anything about playing pranks, had she? She'd talked about her own Goddess, the Golden Sphinx... and she clearly had some magick of her own, what with visions and making that beacon on the oak tree and setting up the third switch on the compass. He'd kept having the feeling like she was hiding something, though...

Well. He could visit Eyola later on, when he was on his way home. Hopefully with a princess in tow. Someday.

Right now...

The trees ahead almost seemed to part – a mossy, green pathway now seemed to stretch away from where Thony and Amanita (and Twinklestar... and Silverfoot) were stopped. The path was illuminated with a green-ish golden light that filtered down through the leaves and made everything look somehow softer and more surreal than it had just moments ago.

And then the coach appeared.

It was tiny – no larger than a doll's coach, with wheels the size of donuts and the open-topped cabin the size of the picnic basket Girona and Midele had fed them all from. Four miniature horses – no bigger than housecats – pulled the tiny thing, their tack covered with miniscule bells that were making that ringing sound.

The noise settled down as they pranced and pawed their way to a stop at the direction of the doll-sized coachman, who was caparisoned in silver and white and softly pastel shades of lavender and green. The lavender and green reminded Thony of Girona's garish apparel, but somehow *this* outfit was entirely elegant. Where the Eyolan girl was clearly trying to make it obvious that she Was A Wizard and Filled With Magick, this small carriage and coachman almost glowed with a lambent light that evoked moonlight and... snow?... and was certainly magickal.

Doubtless Girona would figure all this out. It wasn't really fair to compare, given that she was still pretty much a kid *(even if she was a kid with really awesome magick)*. Thony doubted he'd have been able to sort out the more elegant and impressive look either.

"Well, Amanita," the tiny coachman was lounging back in his seat, reins held negligently, and one foot propped up. "So, we meet again."

Thony looked at his traveling companion in surprise.

"So, we do," she sounded... both eager and resigned at the same time.

The coachman laughed, as high and tinkling a sound as the tiny bells. "And do you remember the rhyme I taught you?"

"No," she said firmly, but in a tone that suggested the opposite.

The little man shook his head, his fashionably curly silver-gold locks shimmering in the odd lighting. "Lavender's blue, Amanita," the mannikin sang in his high voice. "Lavender's green. When I am king, Amanita... you shall be queen."

The girl winced. "And how long until you're king, Puck?"

"Not long, not long at all," he waved a scolding finger at her. "And you've given my name away to the boy. You know he's supposed to guess."

Amanita heaved a sigh. "He grew up with different stories, Puck. I don't think he'd know–"

"The name of the king of pranksters?" Thony was torn between disbelief and awe. "Robin Goodfellow? *Seriously?*"

The small coachman raised a tiny eyebrow at Amanita. "There you go, making assumptions. Robin is an uncle of mine, actually," he informed Thony in that weirdly serious squeaky tone. "'Puck' is a title as much as a nickname for whichever one of us attends upon the Fairy Queen while we're youths. My own time as the Puck is nearly done." He gave a sharp little nod. "Speaking of whom, Her Majesty Queen Lilysong requests and requires your presence."

And he stood up in the carriage and *threw* something...

...and that *something* flew up over their heads...

...and sparkles cascaded down like a dry, pretty rain...

...and Thony felt *odder* than he ever had before...

"That's better," said a light, baritone voice.

The fairy coach was full-sized now, and the delicate-seeming horses were now fiery-eyed mares, stomping at their traces. And the coachman was a full-sized adult man.

No... it was Thony – and Amanita – who had grown tiny. The trees were unimaginably huge around them now, and a nearby mushroom that Thony hadn't even noticed before loomed as large as the gazebo his mother took tea in during Summers. A drop of water clinging to the underside of a fern looked big enough to drown in, and the fern itself looked like a sturdy ladder.

Thony didn't even want to *think* about looking up at Twinklestar and his – or should that be Amanita's now? – horse.

"Hop into the carriage, kids," Puck invited. Or ordered. And he didn't sound the slightest bit high-pitched. Or squeaky.

Thony looked at Amanita, who shrugged and dismounted.

"What about Twinklestar and Silverfoot?" Thony asked.

Twinklestar informed him that *he* would take care of Silverfoot, and Thony should go on and do what the Fairy Queen's flunky said to do.

"A *flunky,* am I?" Puck said humorously, looking up and behind Thony at the now-giant-seeming unicorn. "We'll have to see about that, unicorn."

Twinklestar's snort of disdain blew Thony off his feet almost before he had noticed that *Puck* understood the unicorn just fine.

A giant, silvery rock, striated in a nearly vertical fashion, suddenly descended beside him in the perfect location to use to haul himself back to standing... no, it wasn't a rock, it was Twinklestar's hoof... and there was a sense of apology from the unicorn...

Amanita had already climbed into the carriage.

With a sense that what little control he had over this adventure had just evaporated entirely, Thony climbed in after her.

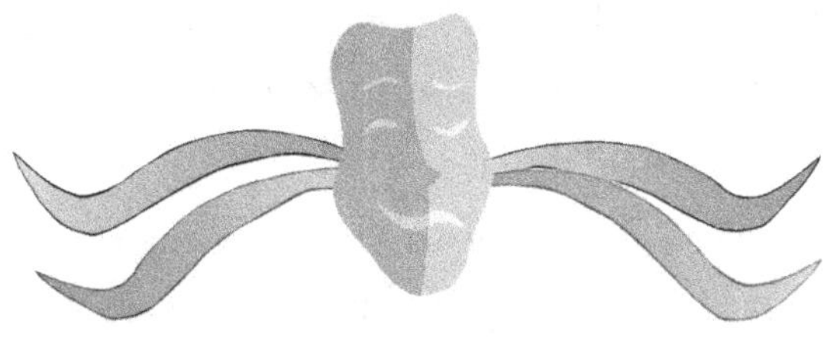

Chapter SEVEN

The Fairy Queen's Court

THE DRIVE TO THE FAIRY Queen's Court was... hard to comprehend. Thony found that there was simply no way to *focus* on any of the things rushing past them; he could catch an impression of something incredibly beautiful and it would be gone before he could figure out what it was. Likewise, he would see something utterly terrifying, but it too would be out of sight before he could try to identify it. Not to mention that the terrifying things also seemed to be unbearably beautiful and the beautiful things held some sort of unspeakable danger in their very existence.

Thony found himself trying *not* to look after a while.

Which was *sort of* easier. The light varied unpredictably and by looking only at their driver and the horses and Amanita inside the carriage with him, he was able to restrain both fear and wonder and keep his discomfort with the whole thing down to a sort of vague nausea. Like motion sickness, only not.

Amanita looked blasé about the whole thing, but he knew her well enough by now to realize that the former stable-girl would put on a show of nonchalance to mask any qualms. Looking cool and competent and in command was her Thing.

Thony supposed it probably should be his Thing, too. It would be useful for the people of Aldyrwald – and their nosy neighboring nobility and royals – to see him that way. Papa didn't really give that impression; Papa was always kind and accommodating, and perhaps just slightly anxious to please, and that clearly wasn't really working to his – or Thony's, or *Aldyrwald's* – benefit at all.

When, at last, they came to a halt in what might be something like a courtyard of the Fairy Queen's palace, Thony's eyes and mind were simply too boggled and overwhelmed to make out a great deal in the way of *detail.*

He was aware that there was a gentle, but pervasive brilliance. Graceful archways and fanciful looking architecture that somehow melded with the trees of the forest around them. The ground was both a mossy clearing and an elegant parquet – or was that inlaid marble?

Thony barely noticed that he had to be helped out of the carriage – nor could he have guessed at who was doing that helping.

There were – he couldn't rightly call them all *fairies*. Some seemed to fit the picture he'd had in his head of what that meant: wings like butterflies or dragonflies or even like bees or... hummingbirds? Clothing that looked like it was made from flower petals and leaves and fern fronds. Shimmers of glitter trailing after as they winged their way about.

But there were also rather more serenely garbed types, some winged, and some whom he instinctively knew he should not look at too closely to tell if those were cloaks or wings. Some who seemed to carry the darkness of the deepest shadows of the Earth with them, and others who seemed almost made of woven light and as insubstantial as Air itself.

"Not many mortals are permitted to see the insides of the Fairy Queen's Court," Puck remarked as he led them past people – *beings* – that were transcendentally ugly and eye-hurtingly beautiful, ones that bore no resemblance to humans, and others that could have been mistaken for any villager back home at first glance.

Though *only* at first glance – Thony took a second one to tell for sure.

"Maybe that's a good thing," he muttered, brain almost stunned into silence in a way he'd never been before. Even his usual internal dialog was hushed.

It was instantly obvious when they entered the Fairy Queen's actual Throneroom.

The space didn't seem to have *boundaries* the way Thony understood the word. He could almost swear that the floor beneath his feet was made of stars and clouds and rainbows and that it extended into the unknowable distance... *forever*.

Looking *up* was something he decided not even to try.

Queen Lilysong herself sat in the crescent of a palely glowing moon. Her wings seemed to be a gossamer spider-silk hung with dew, and her gown was surely clouds. She looked, for one brief moment, like his sisters – the one, and then the other – but then he realized that it was really Mama she resembled. Except... a version of Mama who was infinitely wise and kind and Powerful and who would never faint at anything.

So, not really *Thony's* Mama.

Except there was some feeling that his Mama had all those things inside *her,* too. Where Thony couldn't see them... maybe even where *Mama* couldn't find them. But somehow, he couldn't doubt that all that *strength* and *magnificence* and *beauty* were hers as well.

The Fairy Queen gave him a merry, approving smile, as if he were a pupil who had captured an idea the way she'd hoped he might. Not that any of *his* tutors – except maybe Roger or Jeremy or his sisters, who hadn't *officially* been his tutors in anything – had ever borne such an expression.

"Welcome, my dear young visitors," the Fairy Queen said in a friendly tone. "You are doing things rather in reverse, I see, *beginning* with Quest'sEnd."

Amanita and Thony gave each other a confused look for a moment. Queen Lilysong watched and waited patiently for them to think it through.

"Oh!" the girl said at last. "That's what Girona called Midele's home – the part of Eyola that they were visiting from. Her homeland was Flowericka, and Quest'sEnd is a town or something."

Thony relaxed a little. "I'd forgotten about that." He grinned a little sheepishly. "I was a little distracted by hearing about all the Gods they're connected to. I'd never even guessed there *could* be a God of Pranksters."

"God of *Mischief,* technically," Puck corrected from off to their side. "Destren handles... rather more than just pranks."

"As you would know, nephew," Queen Lilysong said with a tolerant smile.

To the left of her throne, a tall, impossibly slender man gave a small snort and folded his arms. His skin was even darker than Amanita's and hair as pale as the moonlight that stood up like a blaze of fire atop his head.

"My mischief is all in the service of Your Majesty." Puck gave a small, polite bow of acknowledgment to the Queen, but Thony noticed his eyes went warily to the slender man, and to a woman on the Queen's other side who was as pale as the man was dark, with billowing hair as black as the darkest parts of the sky. The woman was just as slender, and clad – as he was – in flowing, brocaded robes over the most elegant warrior's garb imaginable. The woman seemed to be holding herself even more aloof.

Were they the Queen's bodyguards? Did someone like Queen Lilysong even *need* guards?

"Hardly that," the merry-faced Queen disagreed cheerily with Puck. "Though I know 'tis been there when I require it so. But as for these two..." She looked at Thony and Amanita again. "Backwards isn't necessarily a problem in the Fairy Wood if you can retrace your path when it is needful. And beginning at the very beginning isn't really an option for you, given where you began."

Thony looked sideways at Amanita again, but she seemed almost as baffled as he.

"Where... should we begin, then, Your Majesty?" the girl asked. "When you had Puck bring me here last time, you told me I would find what I was looking for on Thony's world. Except all I was looking for was a place to live for a few years until I was more grown up. And that hasn't worked out at all."

"Hmmn," Queen Lilysong's gaze flickered to her two stoic attendants before returning to the young girl. "Perhaps I was wrong. 'Tis been known to happen occasionally. Or perhaps 'tis that events have proceeded upon your own world at a faster pace than expected. You are needed there, child. There are happenings that require your presence and situations that will not be resolved in your absence."

Amanita's chin lifted. "I thought we agreed that most of those things would work out *better* if I was gone for awhile."

The slender, dark-haired woman shook her head, almost in disgust. "This is not the one we need, my Lady. Neither she *nor* the boy."

"Much as I hate to agree with Lady Opalsinger," the man said, his tone a mixture of condescension and obsequiousness. "I must. The reconciliation you seek cannot be imminent."

Queen Lilysong inclined her head, but kept her eyes on Amanita. "No, Lord Aspenheart, but she *is* a part of it. And *he* will have his own part to play. When rain falls, some soaks into the ground and some flows away into the channels that have been prepared. It is yet to be seen whether these two may be *channeled.*"

Amanita exchanged another baffled look with Thony.

"Events proceed proceedingly," the Fairy Queen went on, this time addressing the young humans, if with no greater clarity. "You, Amanita, are *needed* in your home – even had Thony not begun his own Quest, that *need* would have called you home shortly. And you, Thony, you will be a wildcard in the events that are calling Amanita home. The *channels* of Fate may be reset by one such as you, even as they were reset somewhat by Amanita's appearance upon *your* world. Gods and Goddesses as young and new as Joanna and Roger and Priscilla require a bit of a boost sometimes..."

She settled herself on her moon-throne with a small, confident nod. "You may each ask me an unanswerable Question. And then we shall see you on your way to those Events that await your intervention. Until those Events have been resolved, the Fairy Wood will be closed to you for travel."

An *'unanswerable'* question?

Then what was the *point?*

Amanita looked dismayed. "But I don't *want* to go home!" she almost wailed. "I want to go back to Aldyrwald – or *some*where, *any*where else! I've hardly been anywhere at all!"

While Thony could sympathize, this didn't seem like the sort of venue to express such a concern. Even if he hadn't understood half of what Queen Lilysong had told them, it was clear that she had a Quest of some sort for them to complete. And now it appeared that he had no chance to go home unless he did her bidding.

Which would be a great deal more annoying if he hadn't been planning to go to Amanita's world anyways. If the Fairy Queen was turning him about and making him go back to Aldyrwald before he was ready, likely he'd be just as put out as his friend.

"Um, just what are we supposed to do, Your Majesty?" Thony ventured.

Lord Aspenheart snorted derisively again. "You told him to ask an 'unanswerable' Question, Your Majesty. Apparently, he took you at your word."

"You'll figure it out, Thony," Queen Lilysong ignored the man. "As I said, you are the wildcard in the situation. If it helps, though, what you need to do – is something that will come naturally to you, but is something only you can do."

Well, *that* had been a waste of a Question. Thony knew his fairytales well enough to be annoyed with himself, if a little resigned. Answers that were offered like this by magickal Beings were never supposed to make sense or be useful until it was too late.

"Where are we going to come out of the Fairy Wood?" Amanita asked a little grumpily – and that really *shouldn't* be an 'unanswerable' question. "I was aiming us for Quellarie's cottage."

"With the plan of turning right around and taking Thony back home after he'd seen some of the dangers of such travel," Queen Lilysong nodded. Thony gave his 'friend' an outraged look. "You're right about how unprepared he was for this trip, Amanita, but everyone has to start somewhere. You had Quellarie to get you started. Thony has you. But you won't be going back to Quellarie – she won't be there anyways, so it wouldn't do you any good."

Amanita's eyes grew huge. "But Quellarie *never* leaves the area around her cottage. She told me so."

"A crisis has come up," Lady Opalsinger put in in with a dry look at Lord Aspenheart. "One which neither of *us* may handle for Her Majesty. *You,* however, apparently may."

"If you survive to do so," Lord Aspenheart's 'mutter' was obviously meant to be overheard.

"You're frightening Amanita, Your Highnesses," Puck said, possibly overstating the case since Amanita looked baffled, not scared. He came to stand between the young humans and put an arm around each of them. "And confusing Thony. Auntie dear, can't I just catch them up on the way?"

Queen Lilysong sighed. "Amanita has yet to ask me her Question, Puck. Are you truly so eager to leave our hallowed halls?"

Puck chuckled, though it sounded a tad forced. "I've done my turn to bring some laughter here. It's time for someone else to give it a try. It's not just Amanita being called home – as you know."

Thony was beginning to feel like he'd come into the middle of someone else's long-running conversation. He had *no clue* what was going on, but these Powerful Beings seemed to be making decisions about his fate with hardly any regards to his – or Amanita's – preferences. Although the girl at least seemed to have the occasional clue.

"Fine." Amanita put her hands on her hips and glared. Since she was tiny even for a fairy-sized human, it wasn't terribly intimidating. "An unanswerable Question. If I go along with all this *nonsense* and go back *home,* will I get to travel the Fairy Wood again?"

Queen Lilysong brightened up. "Why yes! Should you ever choose to return, there will be a member of my Court ready to assist you in your travels."

Amanita looked surprised and pleased.

But Thony thought there were a few too many 'ifs' and 'buts' in that 'Answer'. Though if Amanita didn't *choose* to return to the Fairy Wood, presumably that would be because she was *choosing* to stay somewhere else. Wouldn't that mean she was *happy* about it? And that would be good, right?

On the other hand, he'd planned to bring her back to Aldyrwald...

Well... chances were that Wesley would find someone else. Eventually. Thony had seen the squires and Mama's ladies-in-waiting fall in and out of 'love' all the time. He wasn't even really sure that he believed there was such a thing as True Love. Well, except for Gods and Goddesses, maybe, because Roger and Joanna... And maybe for *parents,* because Mama and Papa were pretty attached to each other, too...

The Queen had risen from her moon-throne, and now came forwards to place a rather motherly kiss on each of their foreheads. "This will mark you as having My Blessing, children. Should your need arise and there is one of Mine near enough to aid, they will do so. And should the reverse happen, you will yourself feel the call."

Thony figured that was fair.

"*Now* you may take them, Puck. Be well, and give My Love to Snowmistral."

"Mother will be pleased to have it," Puck replied. He laughed. "I do believe I'll miss my time here, Auntie. Though perhaps your next Puck will have better luck with that pair of sour-pusses over there."

Lady Opalsinger glowered at him. "The world is a serious place, prankster."

Puck sketched a bow. "I'll see you at home, doubtless, Your Highness. Perhaps I can persuade you otherwise."

He threw her an impudent kiss, his gaze flickering to Lord Aspenheart as he spun the two young humans around and propelled them back out of the Queen's Audience Chamber with its oddly infinite floors and unbounded edges, one hand on each of their backs.

"Farewell, Auntie – and sourpusses!" he called back jauntily over his shoulder. Surely Thony was only imagining the slight trembling of Puck's hand on his shoulder.

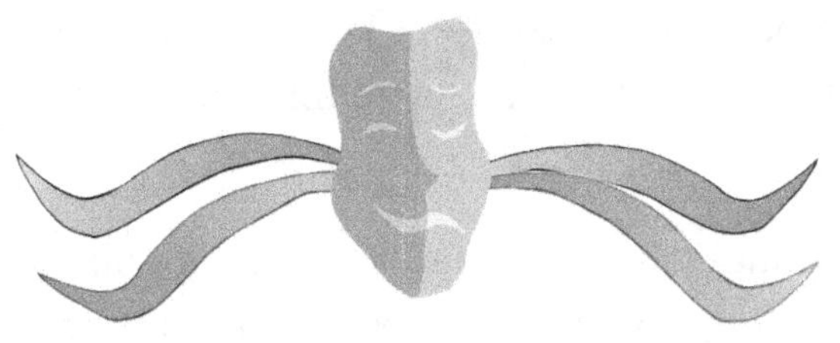

Chapter EIGHT

On the "Road" Again

"WHO WERE THOSE GUYS?" THONY whispered to Amanita when Puck finally strode ahead, a group of fairy-children collecting around him to say goodbye.

"I *think* they were the prince of the Light-elves and the princess of the Dark-elves," Amanita whispered back. "The names match anyways."

"They didn't seem to like each other," Thony noted. "*Or* Puck."

Amanita shrugged. "Maybe he can explain if you want to know. Later."

Quite a bit later, because the fairy-children were laughing sadly as the prankster tickled or poked or teased or hugged them each in turn and by temperament. He was clearly a dear favorite and there didn't seem to be any expectation that he'd be coming back soon.

"Why is he going with us?" Thony whispered to Amanita as they waited in the carriage, watching the extended goodbyes.

Amanita winced a little. "He has to go home, too, he said."

Thony thought back. "That song? He's going back to be a king? And *you're* going to be his queen?" He stared at her in shock.

But the girl waved a slightly irritated hand at that idea. "Don't be silly."

Thony didn't have a chance to ask more questions, though, because Puck had vaulted onto the back of a black fairy-horse that was even more beautiful than the ones pulling the carriage; proud and spirited and... she had *wings*. Dragonfly-like wings. And they had a different coachman, and the carriage was starting to pull away and return down that avenue of horrifying beauty and compelling terror.

They saw Silverfoot and Twinklestar from afar and almost looking like normal – but by the time they came close enough for the fairy coachman to stop and have them debark, the equines loomed again like giants.

Another sprinkling with fairy-dust resulted in Thony and Amanita – and Puck and his horse – growing to human size. The fairy-horse was as pretty as she had been when small, but her wings had vanished.

"Kind of hard to play any good pranks when you're riding a sixteen-hand horse with thirty-foot wings," Puck explained as Amanita and Thony looked quizzical. "Chillabiaen doesn't mind. She's been known to pull her own pranks."

Silverfoot was looking at the fairy-mare with frank appreciation, and Twinklestar was doing his darndest not to look like he was doing the same. Not that either of them would be likely to catch her eye. The horse was a gelding, and the unicorn was practically a pony.

Twinklestar favored Thony with a dark look, apparently having picked that up from his thoughts. This was followed by the distinct impression that a unicorn's maiden was supposed to be on the *unicorn's* side in all matters. The prince gave the unicorn a shrug and tried to think rather pointedly that the whole 'unicorn-maiden' thing was not *his* idea.

Twinklestar looked disgruntled.

"Mount up, kids, we've got a long ways to go," Puck noted as he swung himself into the saddle. "And since *none* of us have wings..."

"Yeah, why don't *you?*" Thony asked, as he reluctantly mounted Twinklestar. "I mean, before anyways. When you were small. All the stories say the Puck is a fairy."

Amanita rolled her eyes. "Because *our* Puck is a *Snow* Fairy, dumbo. They never have wings."

Puck shook his head at her. "Weren't you the one who was telling me he wouldn't even know who I am at all?"

"Well, he doesn't need to be *rude* and ask *personal questions.*" Amanita gave Thony a dark look before looking back at Puck. "You will *never* guess what Prince Nosy-Pants there was asking me about the very first time I met him."

Puck's eyebrows went up.

Thony rolled his own eyes. "I asked about her family. It seemed pretty normal to me."

"Hmmn." Puck looked between them, ending with Thony. "I can see both your points, I suppose. Not that it bothers *me* that I don't have wings. We all use magick to fly anyways. No way could we lift the mass of our bodies without it."

"See?" Thony hissed at Amanita.

"It was still *rude,*" she retorted.

"Was not. He said so."

"Was, too."

"Was not."

"Was, too."

Apparently, this descent into childishness got on even Puck's nerves after a few more repeats, because he and Chillabiaen moved out far enough ahead of the others that Thony and Amanita would have had to yell to make him hear them. It left Thony feeling oddly better, however, and Amanita looked a little less stressed as well.

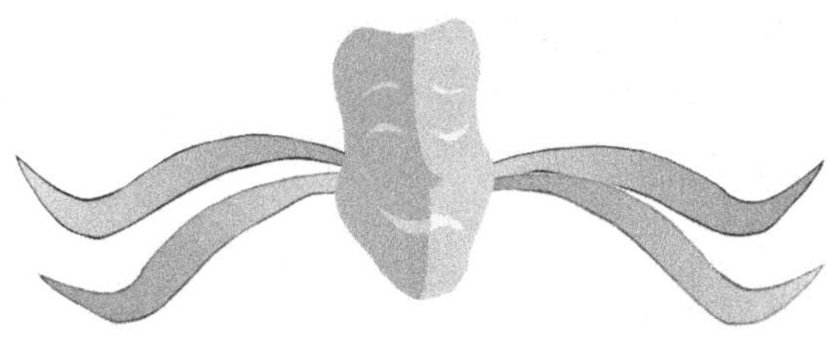

Chapter NINE

Fighting Dragons?!?

"THIS 'ADVENTURE' IS SERIOUSLY BORING," Thony complained to the overhead branches as he lay in his bedroll next to their campfire that night.

"What are you talking about?" Amanita asked. "We got chased by a monster, met people from a world *I'd* never heard of before, visited Fairyland, and got ourselves the King of Pranksters as a guide."

"I never so much as caught a glimpse of the 'monster', those girls were pretty normal, and the visit to Fairyland was interesting, but still pretty tame," Thony replied.

"I thought you were doing this to find a bride, not fight monsters," Amanita reminded him.

The young prince shrugged. "Yeah, I suppose so. Eventually, anyways, I mean. I don't really want to be gone years and years, but there aren't really a lot of options, because I am way too young to get married right now. So, there's lots of time to – I don't know – battle dragons or something."

"You don't *battle dragons,*" Amanita sounded horribly shocked.

"Maybe the dragons on his world are different," Puck volunteered from where he was doing... something to setup for the next morning's breakfast. He was even better at cooking than Amanita, which had left her both miffed and satisfied. No one had suggested Thony try cooking again.

"Dragons are nice here?" Thony asked, feeling vaguely disappointed. He raised himself up on one elbow to be able to look around at both of them.

Not that he had any mad dragon-fighting skills or anything.

Or even any fighting skills at all, really.

Could Puck teach him how to use that sword that was still on Silverfoot's saddle? The oversized fairy-man had a blade of his own, though he hadn't drawn it since he joined them.

Amanita had sat up to hyperventilate more effectively.

Puck was watching her with something like amusement. "The Patron Goddess of our homeland is the Silver Dragon," he explained to Thony. "Most of the dragons in this part of the world are Her Grandchildren."

"Oh." Thony lay back down with a sigh. "So, you have *tame* dragons. I say it again. This whole thing is seriously boring."

"Not *tame,*" Puck said quickly, before Amanita could *actually* explode. "Definitely not *tame.*"

"Sorry?" Thony wasn't really sure what he was apologizing for. It wasn't like he knew these things already or anything.

"Well, you'll get all the excitement you want before we manage to make it back to Pathremir," Puck said casually, settling back into... whatever cooking thing he was doing.

At least he seemed to treat food as seriously as Thony did. The young prince couldn't help remembering that Amanita had been willing to put live frogs into a stew back in the Aldyrwald Royal Kitchens for a revenge prank. Nor that her defensiveness over her containers might have ended up with a seriously bad cake on the royal table. Puck's care with their breakfasts – Amanita was still handling dinners and no one was letting Thony cook – was much appreciated by the young prince.

Not much else deserved such consideration in Puck's opinion, however. And there were some... Thony wasn't sure if he should call them *down-sides,* given that he was a prankster himself, but there were definitely some *differences* in having the king of pranksters traveling with them.

There had been spiderwebs covering the openings of their boots this morning, and the grass-drool-stains on the shoulders of Thony's tunic were now a rather vile shade of puce that apparently even Twinklestar found unpleasant to look at *(though that had the salutary effect of keeping the unicorn from getting close enough to drool on him anymore, so maybe it wasn't so bad)*. And there was something hilarious about Thony's long-overdue-for-a-wash hair, if Amanita's glances and giggles throughout the day had meant something.

Thony had kept his thoughts to himself about the 'kick me' sign that had appeared on her back, since it had seemed more of an after-thought than anything. And he didn't really want to draw attention to himself – though Puck's amused glances at Thony's horse-gelled hair seemed to suggest that he thought the young prince didn't need anything else done to him for now.

But at some point, they were obviously going to have to get Puck *back*...

Amanita's expression was almost comical in dismay right now, though.

"You *told* him."

Puck rolled his eyes. "It's not like it *means* anything to him, Amanita. It's just the name of another place he's never heard of, on a world he's never been to."

That was absolutely true.

"It's not like it'll tell him anything about who you *are.*"

Thony sat up again, fast. "Why? Who *is* she?"

"He already knows your name and it means nothing to him," Puck commented. "It won't matter if he knows the rest."

Amanita was glowering at Puck, who was smirking back at her. "It will once we're out among other people who *know the rest.*"

Puck shrugged unrepentantly. "He'll have to find out eventually. If we're taking him there with us. And since *I* have to go there, and *you* have to go there... were you really planning on ditching him somewhere along the way?"

Amanita's eyes slid over to Thony in a very unreassuring manner. "Noooo...."

Did she seriously think he'd forgotten that Queen Lilysong had told him she'd planned to do exactly that?

The young prince rolled his eyes. "Whatever." He lay back down and put an arm over his face. "You can keep your little secret as long as you like. I'm probably going to have to leave you guys *eventually* anyways."

"Oh?" Puck sounded curious, and Thony uncovered his face to look at the fairy-man.

"Well, you're clearly a prince, if you're going to be a king. But even if you have sisters or cousins or something, I probably need to go somewhere other than a kingdom ruled by fairies to find my princess. Somehow, I think Mama and Papa – and our obnoxious neighbors – are going to insist on a human princess for the next queen of Aldyrwald."

Puck's eyebrows went up again, and he seemed to be smirking. "Oh, Pathremir isn't–"

"He'll see when we get there, Puck, won't he?" Amanita was almost pleading.

The fairy-man snorted. "Are you *actually* hoping he'll meet your grandmothers *before* he finds out who you are?"

She covered her face with her hands. "No. Oh. My. Goddess. That would be the Worst. But... a little bit longer... please?"

Puck shook his head, but let it lie... though now Thony was wondering if *Amanita* was some sort of over-sized fairy, too. A cousin of Puck's? They didn't look enough like to be siblings – not that *he* was a one to speak, though everyone said that he and Joanna and Priscilla's faces were all shaped the same or something.

The idea of Amanita being a fairy-princess was... ludicrous. The girl barely had the manners to make it in a Royal Stable – she'd notably gotten tossed out on her ear from the Royal Kitchens. A fairy-princess would be... more delicate, for one thing. Even at human-size, there was something *different* about Puck. And Amanita didn't have it.

Though if they were related, it would explain how they knew all the same people and why Puck was treating her like a little sister. And why she was putting up with it.

Maybe she was an illegitimate half-human half-sibling of the fairy-prince.

That was an hypothesis worth considering...

Amanita narrowed her eyes at Thony as if she guessed what was running through his mind, then turned her attention to Puck.

"What do you mean he'll get all the excitement he could want before we get home?" She frowned even harder. "Does it have something to do with this crisis that Queen Lilysong mentioned is why we're not starting at Quellarie's house?"

"It might," Puck said without looking up from his work.

Amanita got up and stalked over to him, pulling a... small metal board with lots of... dots?... and a small orange ball out of his hands. "I'm grating the orange peel. You – talk."

They'd had candied orange peel and marmalade and orange-flavored cakes and things at home, but Thony had never seen the fruit itself. He thought he remembered hearing that the fresh fruits couldn't last the journey to Aldyrwald from wherever they came from, so the Royal Kitchens had to make do with preserved versions.

Presumably this was Puck's fruit and he'd obtained it in Fairyland. Though it surely said... *some*thing that Amanita knew what it was.

Puck dusted his hands, then leaned back on them, looking up at her. "How people as quiet and retiring as Ytheril and Naeel ever managed to have a kid like *you...*"

"You can blame my grandmother for that. Both of them. Now *talk,*" Amanita said peremptorily. "Tell us what we're getting into when we get out of the Fairy Wood. And where we're coming out, for that matter. If we're not starting at Quellarie's cottage."

Puck sighed. "We're coming out somewhat east of Brelsin. Do you know where that is?"

Amanita sniffed disdainfully as she carefully rubbed the orange fruit against the metal board. "I *have* had an education. It's east of Sethival. And Selavan. And even of the Plains of Gavenor." She seemed to go a little pale as she said it. "*Very* much east. Why there?"

"Wait, have you been to this place before?" Thony demanded of the girl.

She gave him an irritated look. "Of course not. It barely even counts as a country. Do they even have a queen?" she asked Puck. Thony found it oddly disconcerting that she used the female title as casually, and in the same sense, as he would have said 'king'.

The fairy-man shook his head. "No, and that's part of the problem. Brelsin has always been the sort of place that invading forces pass *through*. It's these dry plains that are a little too rocky to make for good farming. And situated between a half-dozen other lands that take turns invading each other – herding sheep and cattle has been sort of pointless as well. The invading armies just take any livestock for their provisioning. There's a number of small trading towns that more or less get left alone because they provide things the various armies need – like entertainment and the replacement of certain items that are awkward to fix on the move."

"But there's some of the Fairy Wood there?" Thony asked.

Puck nodded. "A few old groves. The Queen acts to protect them so that we have access to the area without having to travel inordinate distances."

"The Wood exists much closer to home," Amanita commented with careful nonchalance, eyes intent on her work of rubbing the orange against the grater. "It seems... *unhelpful* to make us come out there instead of closer to... home."

Puck snorted and got up to rummage around in his packs. "You're the one who didn't want to go *home* at all."

"Nor you," she retorted, and he sighed.

"No. Not yet. Though for more or less the opposite reason as you. As you know."

Well, *Thony* didn't know, for all that *Amanita* was nodding sympathetically.

"Care to clue *me* in?" the young *(human)* prince asked with some sarcasm.

Puck looked ready to answer, but Amanita glared at him, and he sighed again and shook his head. "Maybe later, Thony."

He started arranging bowls and small bags and things on the ground.

Well, *that* was annoying.

"So, we're coming out of the Fairy Wood by this Brelsin-place, and we have to travel across a country that regularly gets rolled over by invading armies, and go how far to get to... *Pathremir?*" Thony asked. He smirked a little as Amanita looked up and narrowed her eyes at him, presumably for remembering the name of her home country.

Their home country. And just *why* had she never mentioned that she was best buds with a fairy-prince? Okay, maybe not in Aldyrwald, when she was trying to blend in, but why not *after* they entered the Fairy Wood? It wasn't like they hadn't had several *days* of travel for her to come clean on something that seemed pretty relevant.

"It's a few weeks of riding," Puck answered as he began measuring things from the bags into the bowls. Flour and sugar and stuff, Thony guessed; white powders, anyways. He accepted the ground up orange peel from Amanita with an absent nod, and mixed it in while the girl began opening the fruit up into pieces. "Assuming we don't get tangled up in the war that's about to start there."

Thony automatically caught the section of fruit that Amanita tossed at him, but his mind wasn't on the squishy, pale orange thing. "We're going through a *war zone?*"

"Mind the seeds," Amanita told him. "They taste terrible and they'll make you choke. I want to know about this, too," she added.

Puck kept his eyes on his mixing. He was adding in fresh eggs now and some sort of liquid from a small flask. "My dear Auntie wants us to check it out. I'm supposed to report on where things stand when we get back to another patch of Wood. To Lady Opalsinger." He made a face as he mixed ingredients. "Auntie can go anywhere she likes, of course, but the Dark-elves and Light-elves don't like to travel very far outside of the Wood. And the groves available in Brelsin aren't big enough to be useful to them."

Thony frowned. "What about you?"

Puck shrugged. "I'm just the Queen's prankster. I can go anywhere, but no one really cares if it takes me a while to get there. If I think I need to go faster, I use the Wood, too, of course."

"But *Queen Lilysong* can travel anywhere she wants – and *she* doesn't need to use the Fairy Wood?"

Amanita rolled her eyes at him. "Why would she?" There was something odd about the way the girl said the pronoun...

Puck was pouring a sort of batter into... a muffin-pan.

"My dear Auntie has a number of other names, Thony. And titles. One of them is the Guardian of the Ways Between the Worlds. As the Waywalker, She is the *source* of the Fairy Wood's Power. She extends its capabilities to the Wood-entire to make travel more convenient for the rest of us."

Thony was beginning to feel like he'd *really* missed what was going on when they met the Fairy Queen.

"The Fairy Wood is a home to the Greater Fae," Puck was going on, "Though many have their own homeworlds as well, most of them have major strongholds here on this one, because Queen Lilysong has created this world as a *cruxpoint* – or... if you were from a more technologically advanced time on your world, either of you, I'd call it a transfer station. Your people, Thony, came from the Hearth-world where humans first arose, came through a WorldGate – *not* the Fairy Wood, since there are a few spots that work better for larger migrations – and then moved on to the world where they are now. The centaurs came from a different world and have spread out almost as widely as humans. And, of course, we have permanent populations here as well. Of many different species."

The mixing bowl was scraped nearly clean, and Puck was now carefully nestling the muffin-pan into the hot ashes of the side-fire he had let burn itself out a bit ago. He looked up with a wry grin at Thony before pulling on some heavy leather gloves and starting to build a structure of hot bricks over the muffin-pan… where had he gotten bricks? He'd picked them up from the fireside, but Thony hadn't seen them there before…

"It's a lot to absorb, and very little of it is relevant to what you really want to know. But Amanita doesn't want to talk about *that.*"

The girl sniffed again, and spit an orange seed into the part of the fire that was still burning merrily. Thony knew her well enough to tell that it was mostly news to her as well, and she was as fascinated as he was. It also looked like she was afraid to ask stuff herself – had Puck never been this forthcoming with *her* before?

"So... if *you're* one of these 'Greater Fae'," Thony began carefully, wondering now what sort of Being he might be offending with his questions, "then what–"

Puck interrupted him with a laugh. "Oh, *I'm* not one of the Greater Fae. Not exactly even Lesser Fae, technically. My people are Elementals, and one of the few groups that are actually *native* to this world. As Elementals always have to be."

"Then Queen Lilysong..." Thony began.

"I call her my 'Aunt' out of politeness," Puck nodded. "My Mother – in Her Aspect as Queen Snowmistral – has been watching over our people for the last couple thousand years or so. But even She is only a Little Sister to the Waywalker."

"Her *Aspect...* a *thousand years...*" Thony gulped a bit. "So, your mother is a... a..."

"A Goddess," Puck nodded again, then looked rather wryly at Amanita. "And despite the Silver Dragon claiming Amanita's people as Her Own, they – *and* their neighbors to the south – are descendants first and foremost of *my* Mother."

Amanita's mouth tightened and her chin lifted. "We don't talk about *those* people. Or *to* them. If we can help it, anyways."

Puck sighed. "They're your long-kin, and both Mother and the Silver Dragon want you reconciled."

"Not going to happen." Amanita looked entirely obstinate in the flickering firelight.

"Amanita, are you really blaming those people for things that their *ancestors* did two thousand years ago?"

The girl crossed her arms. "You know the history of their last three generations as well as I do. They haven't changed."

"Your own mother and grandmother think they have. And there are *reasons* to make peace with them." Puck hesitated. "Two *thousand years*. Don't you think–"

"*Some* things can *never* be forgotten or forgiven." The girl got up and went over to her bedroll, lying down facing away from the rest with an audible thump.

Which likely hurt a bit, since the ground was pretty hard.

She was an overly stubborn creature and bit too inclined to hold grudges. Twinklestar had broken off his continued not-so-discreet admiration of the elegant Chillabiaen to share his opinions with Thony. It was conduct unbecoming of a unicorn-maiden; clearly Twinklestar had made the right decision in picking Thony instead.

The young prince gave up on trying to understand *what was going on* and tromped off himself – after securing a chunk of soap from his own saddlebags – to try to scrub his hair out in the nearby stream. The trickle was still small for the job, but it was the largest one he'd seen in days. He was more than a little irritated that neither – *none,* if you included the unicorn – of his traveling companions would give him a simple, straight answer to *anything.*

While hearing Puck's history of where his own people came from – and it was a little hard to believe, because there was a whole huge *world* filled with people beyond the admittedly limited mountain-region Thony was familiar with – had been *interesting,* it wasn't exactly *useful.*

Well, perhaps except for the notion that Queen Lilysong was actually some sort of SuperGoddess that all the rest kowtowed to.

Which made it all the more embarrassing to think about how *weird* his hair had been when he met her. Thony didn't think he was particularly *vain,* but he *did* have better manners than to show up before some sort of SuperGoddess with his hair dried into all sorts of weird spikes with greenish horse-drool.

And... it also sort of put paid to his idea that Joanna and Roger – and maybe Priscilla – could come rescue him, even on another world, if he got in over his head. I mean, they were *Gods,* after all, so it had made a certain amount of sense.

But they were Elemental Gods. And from Puck's description, Queen Lilysong ranked *everyone,* but especially Elementals... who also seemed to be limited to Their Own worlds, possibly.

And the Fairy Queen – who was clearly *so much more* than some pretty flitterby thing the way the stories had her – had told him and Amanita that they had to visit her homeland and do some Stuff before they were *allowed* to travel in the Fairy Wood again.

Before Thony was *allowed* to even try to go home again, whether he found a princess or not.

And likely there was a *war zone* they had to make it across.

It was all far more profoundly disturbing than he had anticipated.

The soap and cold streamwater weren't making a great deal of headway against the dried horse-drool... any more than his thoughts were making much headway against the situation he found himself... *immersed* in.

Perhaps things would wash out better in the morning – hair and hopes both.

And perhaps he could make himself get up early enough to hunt for some frogs for Puck and Amanita's bedrolls. They both clearly deserved that for continuing to leave Thony in the dark about... even the stuff they were *actually* discussing in *front* of him.

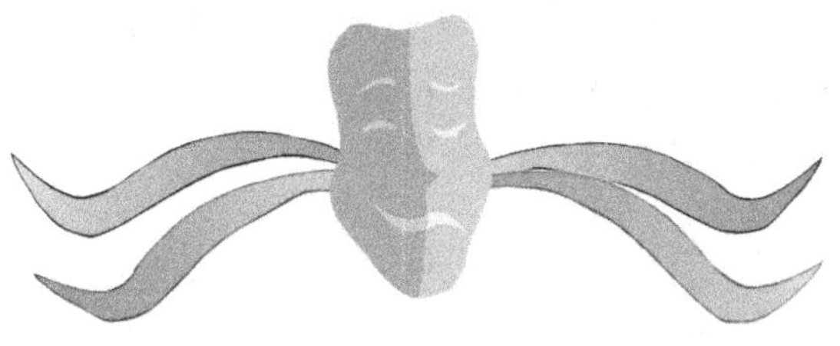

Chapter TEN

The Dress

ORANGE-CRANBERRY MUFFINS AND PAN-FRIED SAUSAGE were *almost* enough to make Thony feel guilty about the hilarious noises the other two had made when they felt the chill, slimy skin of the frogs in their bedrolls.

He had managed to get up, wash out his hair and clothes – and take a quick spongebath – then find the frogs and finish his work while the other two were still deeply in dreamland. The equines had watched him with, hmmn, *equanimity,* but he'd rather thought Chillabiaen looked amused.

The good thing about traveling with other pranksters was that no one took these sorts of things hard. Not that anyone had believed Thony's protestations of innocence *(he'd managed to get back into his bedroll before the fun started)*. There were a few rueful 'good one' comments, and some averted eyes that seemed to suggest they both knew why the young prince had been annoyed enough to prank them.

Not that it appeared to do any good in eliciting enough guilt that they were actually going to *tell* him the things he needed and wanted to know.

Not now, anyways.

Not *yet.*

It might take a few more pranks to make his point.

But it appeared they'd have time. Thony had done the math in his head. A 'few weeks' of riding meant somewhere between three hundred and well over a thousand miles, depending on exactly how long they were talking, and what kind of a pace they could set. His money was on the larger numbers, given that it sounded like the area they'd be traveling seemed to see a lot of travel. Invading armies should leave hardpacked and smoothed 'roads' behind them, shouldn't they? So that should mean they could just ride along at a good clip and cover a lot of distance.

Thony's imagined adventure had run along the lines of learning to fight dragons *(apparently Not the Done Thing here)* and discovering long forgotten castles with secret treasures.

Dodging armies in a *war zone* had not even been on the *list.*

The very words 'war zone' seemed to make everything sound scary instead of exciting. Thony had never been what one might call a 'serious student of history' – and the mountain-region that contained Aldyrwald wasn't really set up for massive wars of conquest. However, until some five hundred years earlier, all the various little countries in the region had regularly invaded, sacked, burnt, and conquered each other for any excuse under the sun. His tutors had mostly avoided texts describing those times, but Thony had dug a few up to satisfy his own morbid curiosity. Even in what was clearly the Bowdlerized written descriptions prepared by some bard to toady up to whichever petty king had triumphed, there had been enough blood and gore and horror to make him want to avoid a return to those days with all his heart and soul. When he'd put the book aside, Thony had sworn to himself to never, ever, ever let Aldyrwald fall to those ancient, evil ways... no matter what he had to give up to protect it.

It had been, his then-eight-year-old-self thought, a proper sort of oath for the Crown Prince of Aldyrwald to make.

And... he was living that *now,* by having fled Aldyrwald before their neighbors decided to descend in a feeding frenzy to declare the Devinthal family to have lost the Divine Right of Kings. At least, Thony *hoped* his absence would prevent that disaster by necessitating his brother-in-law, Roger, being named Heir to the Throne. Which would mean Roger's own father, King Richie, would have to support the Devinthals or risk being put into the same category...

And with Schwannsberg standing alongside Aldyrwald, that should be enough might to at least defer, if not permanently deter their greedy neighbors' ambitious plans. Possibly the kingdoms of the princes that Roger's eldest and youngest sisters were marrying – and the one where Roger's youngest brother was currently supposed to be 'rescuing' a princess-Heir – would stand with them as well, though that might be too much to expect.

Still, Schwannsberg had two valleys, and Aldyrwald had three, with all the prosperity and knights that implied. Perhaps Thony's five knighted middleborn uncles would even come home to help.

Things should be fine...

Though not forever, since Roger and Joanna had other responsibilities than Aldyrwald.

It was Thony's job to find a better solution than marrying one of the middleborn princesses from a country bordering

Aldyrwald with the caveat that her homeland would get one of Aldyrwald's valleys in return. And that the entirety of his kingdom would be ceded to the other king in the event of Thony's death without an Heir.

With that much temptation, Thony wouldn't have long to live after he was wedded.

And even if the princess' country played fair instead of having him *(and Papa)* immediately assassinated following the wedding, just the mere *rumor* that a super-sized country was about to be created might well bring down the pre-emptive wrath of all the rest. Currently Aldyrwald – at three valleys – was one of the larger mountain kingdoms. Combining it with a neighbor via marriage and death would create a four- or five-valley kingdom – as powerful as Aldyrwald and Schwannsberg together, but combined under one ruler more permanently...

Dangerous...

Thony *had* to get home. And he *had* to find a princess-bride so that he was no longer on the marriage-market. *And* he had to find some way to convince all the neighbors – none of whom yet believed that Joanna and Roger and Priscilla were now Gods – that the Devinthals still had the Divine Right of Kings. Not that he had even the tail-hairs of an idea about how to accomplish that last one.

First things first, which meant meeting Queen Lilysong's requirements so he could even *get* home. Eventually.

Puck caught his attention as Thony packed his belongings.

"Thony, you need to change into this."

Against his better judgment, Thony caught the packet of glisteny white fabric that the fairy-prince threw at him. He stood up and shook it out to look at.

It was a dress.

A glisteny, white, long dress with a full skirt and long, draping sleeves.

It sort of reminded him of the outfit that Eyolan girl, Midele, had worn. Because she was a novice priestess, she had said.

He looked at Puck incredulously, just as Amanita began 'trying' to smother a giggling fit.

"You're kidding."

Puck shook his head, a smirk playing around the corners of his mouth. "Nope. Twinklestar decided you're his unicorn-maiden. No one messes with unicorn-maidens. Or their traveling companions. We're heading across a possible war zone, and making it clear we have a bonded unicorn is our best bet for safety. This is what unicorn-maidens wear, so... you're wearing it."

"I'm not a *girl,*" Thony pointed out in his most reasonable tone of voice – if through gritted teeth. "No matter what *Twinklestar thinks.* I am *not* wearing a dress."

Twinklestar made it clear that he was under no illusions that Thony was a girl. However, this *was* the traditional garb for a unicorn-maiden, and really humans all draped themselves in layers of fabric all the time anyways, so what difference did it make anyhow?

Puck rolled his eyes. "You clearly still have some growing to do, but you're not shaving yet. Once you're wearing the dress no one will be able to tell."

Amanita burst into fresh gales of laughter – which, given that she was trying to cover it up rather unsuccessfully made her sound like she was dying in a particularly gruesome manner. If one didn't look at her.

Thony spared her a glare just for herself. If she hadn't done – whatever it was – to annoy Twinklestar, it would be her in the stupid dress. And that would at least make *sense*.

"At least it's not *me* having to wear that dress," the girl managed between snorkeling snorts. "Can you imagine how stupid *I* would look in it?"

"Amanita..." Puck said with a sigh.

Thony balled the awful thing up and threw it at Puck's head. "*You* wear it!" he yelled and dashed off to climb the nearest tree.

Amanita was now *actually* rolling on the ground, laughing and making – now it was rofling noises.

Puck pulled the dress off his face and stalked over beneath the branch Thony had made it up to – some fifteen feet up. He glared up at the red-headed young prince.

"Anthony Devinthal. You are *going* to wear this dress if I have to get the tree to bring you down here and hold you in place while I put it on you."

"I'll just rip it off again," Thony threatened furiously. "It's bad enough that Twinklestar isn't even as large as the pony I rode when I was *eight... and* I look ridiculous riding him *anyways*. I am *not* wearing a *dress* and pretending to be a *girl.*"

Puck narrowed his eyes. And looked at the tree. And then his eyes widened in surprise.

"Hunh," the fairy-man said thoughtfully. "Well, apparently *that* won't work."

"I told you so," Thony said, triumphant but suspicious.

Puck waved a hand distractedly. "Oh, you're still wearing the dress. No, it's the tree. The dryad says she won't help." He glanced around the forest. "None of the dryads will."

Thony wasn't sure what to make of that, but Proper Princely Behavior was always to thank someone for their assistance. "Thank you," he whispered to the tree branch, even though it made him feel almost as stupid as the idea of wearing that *dress*.

The leaves on the branch shivered, slightly, though the branch was still and he felt no breeze. A response? Just in case, he patted the branch awkwardly, and saw the leaves move again.

Weird.

"It must be because of those Eyolan girls we met," Amanita suggested, sitting up and dusting herself off. "One of them was part-dryad. Maybe she did something to tell the trees to be nice to us."

Puck gave her another thoughtful look. "They say it's just him."

Amanita's eyebrows went up, and Thony felt his face going red.

Good grief.

"I spent more time talking to Midele," he muttered. "*You* spent all your time talking to that Girona."

"Yeah, that's probably it," Amanita said in that casual, inflection-less way she had that meant she was storing it up to tease him about later. Well, at least she wasn't going to do it in front of Puck. Which was, honestly, all he could really hope for.

"Girona gave me a couple of things, too," Amanita went on, surprising him. "So, it makes sense that Midele would have done the same for Thony."

Puck raised an eyebrow, then shrugged and looked up at Thony in the tree. "Look, kid, I don't need the dryad to help me with this. I can cast a spell to *make* you come down here and put the dress on. And *keep* it on. I just don't like to do it that way."

Thony gritted his teeth again. He didn't like the sound of that either.

But there was a *principle* at stake here.

"That's the only way it's gonna happen," he averred.

Puck sighed heavily. "Alright. This is going to hurt me as much as it hurts you..."

Thony rather doubted that.

But just before Puck did – whatever it was he was going to do – Twinklestar came over and nudged the fairy-man in the shoulder-blades with his velvety nose.

And when Puck turned around to look at the unicorn, he had to look *up* instead of *down.*

Twinklestar was now – somehow – the size of a full-sized horse.

Which was probably just as well, or that *nudge* in Puck's back would have gotten him impaled on Twinklestar's horn. Instead, the pearlescent spiral with it's deadly-sharp tip had gone over the top of Puck's shoulder.

He'd left green drool behind, Thony noted with a certain savage pleasure.

Both magickal beings looked up at Thony together.

Twinklestar made it clear that his new form was intended as a compromise. His sort of unicorns didn't prefer to be this large, but they could be if they liked. Since his size had been one of Thony's complaints, maybe *now* the young prince would put on the white robe and they could get on with things?

Thony felt a little bad at having made Twinklestar feel bad – but given that Puck's fairy-mare was now eyeing the unicorn with a great deal more interest, he suspected that Twinklestar had a secret agenda.

There was nothing wrong with swatting two flies with a single swish of one's tail, Twinklestar gave him to understand. But if *he* was willing to give up something important about himself to make the whole party safer and Thony more comfortable... well, then, shouldn't Thony be willing to make a similar sacrifice?

"Well, kid?" Puck asked. "Looks like this takes care of *one* of your complaints."

"Fine," the boy said aloud. "But we're calling it a *robe* and I'm wearing *real* clothes underneath it."

Rather ungraciously, Thony slithered out of the tree, snagged the *robe* from Puck, and stalked behind a bunch of leafy bushes.

He discovered almost immediately that the stupid thing wouldn't *fit,* and made a trip back out to retrieve the scissors from his saddlebags. He'd brought them along to keep his hair trim and cut threads when he had to do minor repairs on his clothing. Needing to slice a unicorn-maiden *robe* down the front had never occurred to him.

His hair, Thony noticed irritably, probably *could* use a trim. But likely Puck would insist he not. So that Thony would look more like a *girl.*

The stupid *robe-thing* was brushing the ground as he stalked back out, to where Amanita and Puck and Twinklestar were examining the saddle that Twinklestar *had* been wearing.

"There's a belt," Puck said absently, handing it back without even looking. "No, I don't think we can make this work."

Assuming that Puck was referring to the saddle, and not the outfit, Thony took the 'belt'. It was really a *sash,* made of some sort of cloth-of-gold, and it was about four times too long, probably intended to do some girly-sort of dangling job. He looped it around himself twice and tucked the ends in for a sort of cummerbund look.

"The saddle won't fit?" he asked, as he tied the 'belt'.

Puck shook his head regretfully. "Maybe it would have changed with him, if he'd been wearing it while he changed. *Some* kinds of transformation take the clothes along." He waved a hand at Chillabiaen, comfortable in *her* saddle while Thony thought about how they'd all changed size going to and from the Fairy Queen's Court... and decided he was kind of grateful that he hadn't known – *then* – that there were some kinds of transformation that *didn't*.

Twinklestar whuffed with disdain. Equinoids were not meant to wear *clothes*. Though he could see that they did so as a favor to these lesser creatures who needed them so badly. The last seemed to be added on with an embarrassed look at the fairy-mare.

Presumably unaware of this – or at least, Twinklestar's comments *seemed* to be directed solely to Thony – Puck shook his head again. "Sorry, Thony. You'll have to ride bareback. Not but what that isn't the *traditional* way for unicorn-maidens to do it anyways. I'll use a spell to put the saddle... someplace we can retrieve it later."

Thony looked up at Twinklestar, aghast. The unicorn's paces had been jarring and uncomfortable, even *with* a proper saddle and stirrups.

Puck finally noticed how Thony was dressed, and gave him a headshake of his own before coming over and tugging the *robe* closed in the front. Somehow, he got it to overlap a bit so it looked like a dress again. And the sash got unwound so it did the dangly thing.

Thony scowled.

"Unicorn-maidens are supposed to be *modest* and *demure,* Thony," the fairy-man 'explained' as he worked. "You have to look the part."

"I'm wearing a bloody shirt and pants underneath," Thony complained. "I'm practically roasting. Tell me how I could *possibly* be more *modest?*"

"Well, I could use a spell and fix the dress, and then you could take off a few layers," Puck suggested.

Thony grabbed his, erm, *skirts* and stepped hastily away. "Don't you dare. And it's a *robe.*"

He looked up at Twinklestar again. "Bareback. Gods. At least it doesn't have to be *side-saddle.*"

He faltered as he looked at Puck again. "Oh, my God. I don't have to ride *side-saddle?* Do I?"

Puck winced. "That's sort of traditional, too. And... considering that you're riding bareback, maybe it's a good thing?"

Thony thought about the unicorn's spine, and no saddle, and... couldn't really disagree.

Dammit.

"It's going to slow us down, though," Amanita noted. "If he has to ride side-saddle, I mean."

"We wouldn't be going terribly fast with him bareback either," Puck told her, exchanging a sympathetic wince with Thony over the idea. "No stirrups," he told the girl when she gave them a blank look. Not that that was the real answer, but it was true enough.

"Hunh." Amanita folded her arms. "Maybe it's not worth it. If we're traveling through a war zone, doesn't getting *out* faster make more sense? Especially now that Twinkie's big enough to really run with the other equines?"

Puck raised his eyebrows as Twinklestar looked offended and Thony was given to understand that he could put them all to shame no matter *what* size he chose to be.

"And how do we explain the *boy* on the unicorn?"

She waved a dismissive hand at this. "Twinkie was going to illusion away his horn when he agreed to be *my* mount. He can just do that now."

Puck looked at the unicorn in surprise. "You were really going to do that?"

Twinklestar looked rather embarrassed.

"Is it a big deal?" Thony asked. "I don't know much about unicorns."

"A very big deal," Puck sounded impressed. Or amused. It was hard to tell which with him, especially since he was usually impressed if something particularly amused him. "Unicorns don't hide their horns, as a rule. It's one reason why half-breeds like Quellarie are respected, but not accepted. When she's in her other forms, she doesn't have a horn at all."

Which... explained about *half* of what Thony had wanted to know, even if it just raised *more* questions.

A bit better than par for the course with his questions lately, actually.

"You *really* wanted to go with them," Puck mused, still looking at Twinklestar. "But you left with Amanita, not with Thony... And you went to Thony's world with Priscilla in the first place..."

Thony winced as Twinklestar gave him a sideways look and a demand to explain.

"He says he came back with Prissy and the others because she was *almost* right. Except she was obviously *wrong,* since she fell for Jeremy within – hours? Days? Something like that – of meeting Twinklestar. A unicorn and his maiden are supposed to have *years* together..." He looked curiously at the now-huge Twinklestar – he'd made himself at least eighteen hands high. "Not forever? Really? Okay..."

That had been a component of Thony's discomfort with the whole idea. After all, eventually he had to go back home to Aldyrwald, marry some princess, and produce an Heir. None of which squared with being a unicorn's 'maiden'. All the other issues aside.

"He says Amanita was *almost* right also... and *now* he thinks they were both *almost* right because they were close to *me*. Prissy because she's my sister, and Amanita, because we spent a lot of time together. It really wasn't all *that* much time," Thony told the unicorn. "I talked to her like, twice while she worked in the kitchens, and caught sight of her maybe a dozen other times. I actually saw more of her after she was working in the stables and Tad moved me up to riding Silverfoot."

The unicorn gave a twitch of the skin on his withers that was the equivalent of a horsey shrug. Clearly, he didn't need a more detailed explanation for what seemed plain-as-day to him. Now anyways.

Amanita was giving Thony an odd look. "You 'caught sight' of me a dozen times in the kitchens? What were you doing? Lurking around waiting for me?"

Well, *that* made it sound pretty creepy.

He shook his head hastily, even though that sort of *had* been what he was doing. After the first frog incident, he'd thought both that she might be interesting enough to make friends with and also that she might need someone to watch out for her. Which *had* turned out to be true, after all.

"I've always kept a close eye on the kitchens," he said more or less truthfully. "There's a great deal of opportunity there, after all. And, I mean, *you* know the Chief Cook. The man bears watching."

None of which she could really object to. Though, honestly, Thony's observation of the kitchens the last couple of years had been more to de-rail *other* pranksters' tricks from keeping dinner from getting served on time.

He looked back at Twinklestar, who was eyeing him with some apprehension – or at least nerves, after his own explanation had gotten sidetracked.

So, you came for **me?** Thony tried to talk to the unicorn in actual words inside his head for the first time. *Not for Amanita?*

Twinklestar nodded a little hesitantly. He still hadn't been entirely sure, the unicorn admitted. And... he hadn't really believed that a *boy* could be pure enough of heart to be a unicorn-maiden. Not that he *dis*liked Amanita – or Priscilla. But Priscilla as Goddess of Fertility *(the unicorn didn't bother dancing around the truth the way Thony's parents – or even Thony – did)* had been a Very Bad Match, despite her essential purity and innocence. And Amanita...

He didn't seem to have an explanation for why it hadn't worked out with Amanita.

Thony wondered if those grudges she seemed to be holding against her people's nearby neighbors might have been the difference, and Twinklestar allowed as how that might have been a *part* of it... but there was still something else...

Not that it mattered. It was *Thony* he wanted as his bonded 'unicorn-maiden' until Thony was ready to marry his princess. They would just be 'best bros'... if Thony was up for it, anyways.

A wash of relief spread over the young prince. This *wasn't* irrevocable. And he had a *choice*. It wouldn't stop him from fulfilling his responsibilities to Aldyrwald... and, honestly, being chosen by a unicorn was probably the most magickal thing ever going to happen to *him, Thony, personally*.

Even if he had to wear a stupid white *robe*.

Twinklestar nudged up and Thony put his arms around the unicorn's proud neck.

"Well, that's all settled then," Puck sounded relieved as well. "Don't worry, Thony, once we get out of Brelsin, you can probably quit using the dress."

Amanita snorted. "Yeah, right. Because they will be so understanding in places like Sethival. And in Pathremir they will *love* the whole story... but they'll want to see him in white." She gave Thony a sympathetic look. "Maybe a white robe will work, though. Boys dressing up like girls... doesn't go over really well at home." She winced for some reason.

Puck helped Thony – and his dress – get up on Twinklestar's back. How much of the lift was magick and how much was muscle, the young prince really couldn't say. He was just utterly embarrassed about needing the help and resolved to look for rocks, branches, fences... *anything* that kept him from having to be picked up and put on Twinklestar's back like some precious maiden. No matter what impression they were trying to give at a distance.

"You look nice," Amanita offered as they rode along in Puck and Chillabiaen's wake.

Thony ignored her. He darned well *should* look nice in her opinion. She'd spent a good *five minutes* doing *something* to his hair at Puck's direction. Which Thony had felt was utterly *beyond* what he had agreed to, but... in for a lamb, in for an ewe. It had seemed rather pointless to argue, so he had suffered in silence.

And he would continue to do just that.

"I'm... sorry I laughed," she said contritely when he didn't respond. "It was just – your *face.*" It sounded like she was grinning in memory. "I haven't seen anyone look that outraged since... maybe since the Chief Cook fired me."

Thony kept his eyes straight ahead and his face impassive.

"Come on, Thony. How long are you going to stay mad?"

He tightened his mouth and didn't look at her.

He was wearing the *dress* and she'd done his *hair* and he was riding bloody *side-saddle*. He probably looked about as stupid as she'd imagined. Involuntarily, he glanced down at the glistening white fabric that covered his lap and cringed. Some of his hair – in its new, looser style *(and he had no idea how she'd done anything with it, it wasn't* **that** *overgrown)* – flopped into his face, and he shook it back with another cringe, not daring to let go of the reins that were the only thing he had to grab hold of anymore.

"Oh..." Amanita sounded like she'd had a revelation. "You... It's that comment about how I'd look stupid in the dress. That wasn't about you. I hate long dresses. And that one was clearly way too long for me. It drags on the ground when *you* walk, and you're taller."

She paused.

"*Much* taller," she added hopefully, likely remembering that Thony had gotten a little sensitive about his lack of height recently.

However, that was just *true,* and it didn't really mean anything.

"There's, um, lots of stories about girls – princesses – cutting their hair and dressing up like boys," she pointed out after a few more minutes of silence. "And, like, you know, pretending to *be* boys to learn to be warriors. Or knights. Or... to do whatever. It usually falls apart when they start turning into women with, you know, bosoms and stuff. But they usually did some pretty amazing things before that. And sometimes afterwards, too. You're just... writing the story differently."

Thony couldn't avoid a bit of a snort. Despite his resolution, he looked at her out of the corner of his eye. "I thought girls did *all* the fighting where you come from. In *Pathremir.*"

She winced a little, but looked relieved. "Yeah, about that. Sorry. There wasn't any real reason not to tell you. Just... if I mention it on the *other* side of the Fairy Wood there's gonna be all kinds of trouble, so I... sort of got into the habit..."

He snorted again, and she winced again. "Yeah, it was still dumb. And... yeah, girls do most anything in Pathremir. But there's lots of boys who become warriors, too. Even there. They get a little taller, on average, and they seem to get muscly faster, so... and there aren't a lot of other options for them if they want to do something other than be husbands and fathers. And *brothers.*" Something about that word made her roll her eyes. "So, a bunch of them join the military. Not that they get to be officers, past a certain rank, but... they do join."

"You said your father is a shepherd," Thony found himself saying. If she was *finally* going to tell him some stuff, it was probably worth getting over his snit. He'd be traveling in this get-up for days, after all. Maybe *weeks*... or even *months*. He tried not to think about the possibility of *years*.

Twinklestar flicked an apologetic ear at him.

"So did your brother join the military?" he asked.

She hadn't actually *said* she had a brother... but she let Puck treat her like a little sister... And Thony had picked up on a number of mannerisms that he knew he had himself. All that bossiness probably had more to do with this crazy *matriarchal* culture of hers than anything.

Amanita shook her head. "No. He wanted to – though more to get away from home than anything. But Grandmother said he couldn't." She looked... guilty. "She said we all had to stay close to home. For safety."

An anxious old woman got to decide for everyone in the family? That sounded fairly awful.

"Which grandmother?" Thony asked. "The one you kind of like or the one you really don't?"

Amanita gave him a startled look. "You remember that conversation? The one I like. My mother's mother. Of course."

"Why 'of course'?" Thony asked.

She gave him an uncomfortable look. "I'd... still rather not say. What you don't know, you can't accidentally tell. And... we're coming out of the Fairy Wood really soon – where it actually *will* matter."

That was... a little offensive, given that she *knew* that Thony could keep a large number of details straight for a prank and only reveal the proper ones to the proper people. Or... maybe this really did worry her to the point where she was paranoid.

And – for all the Gods' sakes – *why?*

What possible reason could there be not to explain why her grandmother – presumably the matriarch of her family in a girl-obsessed culture – got to make life-decisions for everyone? It seemed reasonably straightforwards...

But since Amanita looked really worried...

And since she *was* his friend. And his guide on her world *(although not his* ***only*** *guide now...)*

Thony relented and gave her a shrug. "Whatever. I guess it's going to be a few weeks or a month or something until I actually *meet* this over-protective grandmother of yours, so there's time."

Amanita looked an odd mixture of pensive and relieved at that thought.

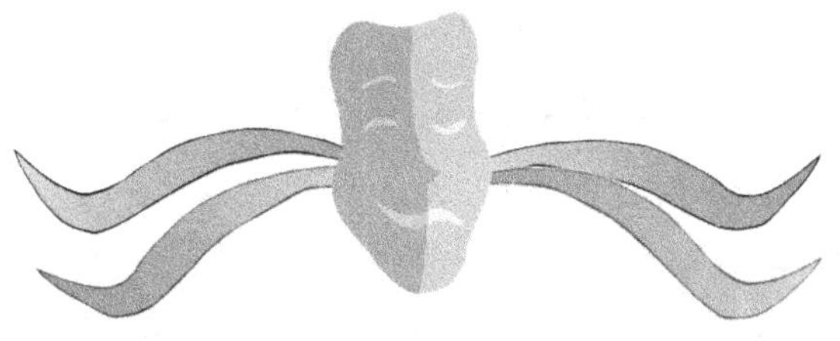

Chapter ELEVEN

Out of the Woods…

THEY CAME OUT OF THE trees shortly before sundown.

The forest had begun to darken, though it felt early to Thony, and he'd been anticipating one or the other of the 'experienced travelers' suggesting it was time to make camp.

Instead, the trees went from humungous to merely large, and the gaps between them were filled with saplings and other undergrowth. Their surroundings seemed to grow *brighter* instead of *darker,* despite the lengthening shadows, and gaps in the canopy of branches showed a brilliantly blue and cloudless sky.

And then, almost abruptly, they were coming out of the trees onto a... well, it was the flattest place *Thony* had ever seen. Hills, he supposed, but they weren't really *hill*-hills. More like a waviness of the land with occasional protuberances.

You could see an unimaginably far distance, since all that seemed to be anywhere – other than behind them – was *grass.*

It was... unbelievably boring.

Green grass, blue sky, and... nothing else.

After a few moments of staring at it – they'd all come to a stop after emerging from the last of the trees and underbrush – Thony began to see that there was a bit more detail to be made out.

The grass was that particular shade that one only sees in fairly early Springtime, and the air was chilly enough to agree with that assessment. Which was interesting in and of itself, since it had been early Summer when they'd left Aldyrwald. Joanna and Priscilla had said something about the seasons not lining up properly on their Quest also... and Amanita hadn't been sure how old she was when he met her... so maybe this was just something else odd about the Fairy Wood.

But now that he was looking, Thony could see small, but brilliant, patches of scarlet; a blue even more vivid than the overly-wide open sky; white that would rival the non-existent clouds; and other bright yellows, oranges... He'd never been allowed to explore the mountains around Aldyrwald's main valley, but he'd watched the profusions of Spring flowers blooming on the distant slopes and had always loved it when the knights and squires took the ladies-in-waiting out to pick flowers. The castle had been filled with bouquets and posies – everything from tall stalks of lavender and misty sprays of baby's breath to vivid orange poppies, golden sunflowers, and purple lupines and delphinium. His favorites had always been the shy little white adelweiss flowers that only rarely made it into any of the formal, public arrangements; those were reserved for courting couples... and that offered a plethora of opportunities to a certain prankster prince.

Not that he'd *really* messed up anyone's romances... at least not without having a plan to fix what havoc he'd caused...

Except for the handful of squires and knights – and ladies – about whom he had no other way to warn their potential romantic partners. *Those* particular people had also been the targets of some of his other subtle efforts, and all but one had migrated on to other courts or – in one case – a marriage, before causing too much trauma to the Devinthals' Court. It was Thony's place to look out for his People, after all.

Some of the plants on this... expanse of too much grass and flatness... stood up taller than others – some of that waviness might be due to local concentrations of taller plants over the grass. No trees, though, not unless those distant, darker-green blobs he could see in some of the depressions were more than bushes.

He looked back at the trees they had come out of, seeking a break from that intimidatingly wide blue sky, and was startled to see that the grand Fairy Wood was only a small grove. It seemed... darker and deeper than was probably reasonable, given that he could see sunlight through the more distant branches, suggesting that he could probably ride *around* this little grove in no time flat.

Twinklestar seemed happier about the open expanse than Thony was. Lots of open space to run, and a great deal of grass – which tasted better out here in the sunshine than the mossy stuff and leaves in the Wood.

"I thought you were a forest unicorn." Thony muttered, and got the impression that Twinklestar's people lived on the margin of forest and plains – that was the word for this vast emptiness.

"Are you okay, Thony?" Amanita asked, her dark eyes concerned.

He tried not to cringe up at the sky. "Yeah, sure. Why not?"

"I don't like this much myself either," she confided. "Pathremir is in the mountains – like Aldyrwald. And there's lots of forest. Both the normal kind and the Fairy Wood. This much sky... it seems unnatural."

Thony nodded, relieved that she wasn't going to laugh at him about this. "It's like it's trying to squeeze me into insignificance." He forced himself to sit up straighter and take a deeper breath. "Kind of crazy, right? Master Eswith always said I let my imagination run away with me too much for my own good."

Amanita surprised him by looking thoughtfully up at the sky. She had a sort of 'I refuse to be defeated by a piece of *sky*' look to her posture. "Out here... I don't know. At home, no. The sky doesn't seem to have any particular Goddess looking after it at home, though we have Sylphara, the Lady of Blizzards and Gales..."

She gave Puck a surreptitious glance, for no reason Thony could see. But the fairy-prince didn't seem to notice. They'd all come to a halt when he reined Chillabiaen in, and he seemed to be staring off into the distance with his thoughts somewhere else entirely.

"Out here," she went on after a moment, "Like I said, I don't know. I've heard that there's a Sky-God in the Muana Desert, but that's thousands of miles away... There could be a different one here."

Thony frowned. "If there's a God of the sky anywhere on this world, shouldn't He be honored everywhere? Or... do people in different places call the Gods by different names?" That would make sense, and he thought he remembered Joanna and Roger and Priscilla – and the others, because this had been shortly after Joanna and Roger's second wedding – talking about something like that.

Amanita shook her head. "It's... things are *really different* here, Thony. Puck was telling us how this world is different than other ones – because Queen Lilysong has made it sort of a meeting-ground. A place where you stop on the way to some other world. Quellarie told me about some of this before I went traveling myself."

Thony was about to ask what that had to do with Gods being different, but Puck seemed to have come back to himself with a shake.

"Time seems to have slipped here more than my dear Aunt thought it would," he told them. "The local sylphs say that they've been trying to get word to us for awhile now, but..." He shook his head again. "I need to do some investigating, and *this* is clearly not a locale to hang around in. There's a town nearby. We should be able to get some answers there."

He looked... far more serious than what they were used to.

Amanita and Thony – and a remarkably meek Twinklestar – didn't question, but merely followed Puck as he and Chillabiaen led the way. Somehow his unusual sobriety made it seem the wrong time to quiz him on things.

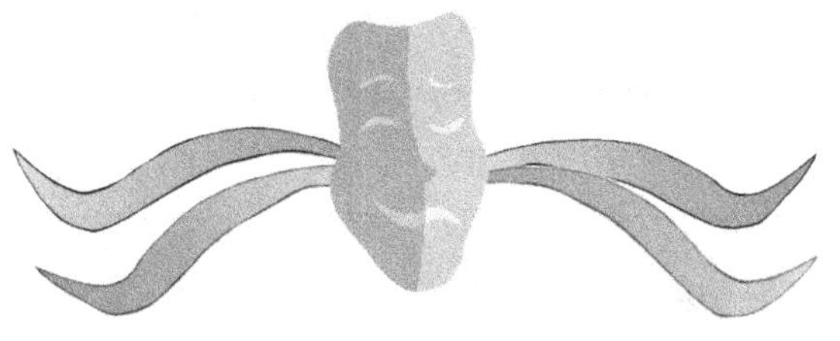

Chapter TWELVE

...and Into Trouble

THE SUN HAD DIED IN a blaze of colors – possibly the most spectacular sunset Thony had ever seen. The faint haze of distant clouds to the west had been painted in oranges and golds and purples and pinks even more brilliant than those occasional patches of wildflowers. One cloud had been a particularly exquisite shade of plum-red.

By extreme contrast, the town they rode into as the blued light was starting to turn into greys and blacks was as dry and dull as... well as the 'Desert Pasture' at home. That had been the 'sacrificial lot' where the dirt had been pounded dead and dry by thousands of sheep and cattle being corralled there before sale in the village market for longer than Thony had been alive.

At this point, the young prince no longer cared.

He'd never ridden bareback for more than a few minutes before, and he'd never ridden *side-saddle* at all. Combining the two had been... awful. Not to mention that they'd stopped a short distance outside of the tired-looking town to remove Twinklestar's bridle and reins. Even if the thing had been a proper hackamore, instead of having a bit, no unicorn would ever abide wearing such a thing.

The fact that Twinklestar *had* – at least while they were in the privacy of the Fairy Wood – was another testament to how badly he had wanted to stick with Thony.

Which Thony now *appreciated...*

... but it didn't make it any easier to ride. Especially now that he also had to cling to Twinklestar's mane and... well, *pray* not to fall off...

The young prince was more than willing to let Puck help him down from the now-tall unicorn at the door to an inn. Silverfoot was already tethered to a hitching post, and Chillabiaen was as well, though the glint of humor in her eye suggested that was only as solid an attachment as she cared to let it be and that she was only putting up with it as part of their disguise.

No one would ever imagine tethering a unicorn, of course.

Puck led the two younger people into the Inn of the Starred Hoof – Thony wincing with every step as his rear end and legs woke back up from having gone numb during the uncomfortable ride. The fairy-man left the younger two close to the door, cautioning them to wait there until he'd had a word with the innkeeper.

"Everyone looks *scared,*" Amanita whispered as they both leaned against the wall.

Or rather, both *tried* to lean against the wall. She was short enough for it not to matter, but Thony's head hit a cloak-hook as soon as he tried. There weren't any cloaks hanging up, it being a fairly mild evening in mid-Spring, so he hadn't noticed before it was too late. He shifted to one side with a wary look at the wall, and rubbed his head before looking around.

She was right – or, at least as right as Thony could tell. Aldyrwald wasn't a place where you saw *fear* in people's faces, so he might have to take her word for it.

The inn was... grungy, was probably the best word for it. The flickering light from the hearth-fire probably improved the look of the place over the candles that were set about at a rather miserly concentration; surely wax couldn't be so dear, not with all those flowers out on the plains!

Less than a dozen men and a handful of women huddled over bowls of food at the trestle tables or nursed heavy-looking mugs at the bar. No one seemed to look anyone else in the eye. A minstrel with hair almost as bright as Thony's strummed some mellow-toned stringed instrument in the corner next to the hearth; her tin cup set out in hopeful expectation seemed empty, the customers ignoring her as thoroughly as they ignored each other.

The entrance of Puck and the two younger people had occasioned a small wave of wary curiosity, but even that had died down almost instantly. All Thony could say for these people was that they seemed just as incurious as the handful of pedestrians they'd seen scurrying along their way during the ride in.

Puck returned quickly, and motioned the two to follow him through a side-door and up some stairs. When Thony asked about food and stabling – and their saddlebags – the fairy-man just shook his head and urged them on.

The second-story of the inn proved to be a long corridor with closed doors on either side. Puck unlocked the second on the right – just over the hearth and the neglected minstrel, if Thony had his bearings right – and ushered them in. He closed and re-locked the door, then walked around the room in a quick circuit, seeming to stare rather intently at the door- and window-frames in particular.

Then he heaved a sigh of relief and waved the other two to sit down.

There was a hearth – cold for now, but with a fire laid for the starting. A small table. Two chairs. Two beds. A few hooks near the door for cloaks. And that was all.

Amanita eyed the somewhat deficient-seeming accommodations worriedly. "Puck..."

"I'll explain what I can. Sit down. The innkeeper is sending food up shortly and we need to get this sorted out as soon as possible."

"All right..." They both said it, then shrugged and settled one to each of the chairs. Thony rather suspected Puck had meant for them to sit on one of the cots so *he* could take a chair but...

Well, maybe not. The fairy-prince fell to agitated pacing as soon as the younger two were seated and the floor was clear.

"It's bad. Not as bad as it *could* be, but bad," Puck told them. "Flowerdust is under the control of the fellow who started this war and–"

"Wait, *what?*" Thony interrupted. "What's 'flowerdust'?"

Did Puck mean that stuff that fell off of flowers – bee-food, Thony had always thought it, given that bees seemed to collect the stuff and take it away to their hives. The Royal Beekeeper had once given him an introduction to his work... followed shortly thereafter by horrified edicts from Thony's parents about how he was never, ever, *ever* to go near the hives again. Thony had never been sure if they were concerned about the risk of him being stung or the potential for havoc. Not that he was likely to mess with something involved in the production of *dessert.*

Puck gave him a distracted look. "It's the name of this town. I've never known if it's because it's surrounded by flowers and actually has more of an industry – raising flowers and honey – than most of the rest of Brelsin, or if it's because everything dries up and turns to dust by the middle of Summer."

Thony nodded for him to go on, and Amanita gave him a quick nod of thanks, presumably for asking the question.

"Anyways, the guy who started the war – an Evil Wizard named Valderon Raven'sWing – is in control of the town. His forces are occupying it as a resupply station is what the innkeeper said, though the Wizard himself isn't here, nor likely to be." Puck looked at them both all-too-seriously. Pranksters – and especially the *king* of pranksters – should never look this concerned. "None of this was supposed to be happening yet. I'm not sure if *we* ended up getting here too late or Raven'sWing got his plans in motion earlier than my Aunt thought he would. Or if he's moving faster than She anticipated.

"But the local sylphs have been in a frenzy since they saw us come out of the Wood – it's why I've seemed so distracted. They don't want to manifest so you can see them, but they've somehow been banned from the Fairy Wood and haven't been able to get through to let anyone know what's happening out here. I have to..."

He sort of seemed to run down as he looked at Thony and Amanita.

"You have to leave us and let Queen Lilysong know what's going on here," Thony said it since Puck seemed reluctant to do so. It was what *he* would feel was his duty in Puck's place... if he understood Puck's place at all.

Amanita looked... slightly alarmed, but not surprised.

The fairy-prince slumped down to sit on one of the beds and nodded despondently. "To Lady Opalsinger, rather. This is the kind of thing she and Lord Aspenheart handle, though probably not *directly*. The Queen doesn't take a direct hand in things very often." He rolled his eyes. "With some very noticeable and recent exceptions down in *Dawil*. Of course, if this were Dawil, then it would be someone else's responsibility entirely. And they have plenty of resources to handle Evil Wizards and such over there. But that's what the Metree– I mean, those people *do*."

Puck cast a worried look at Amanita, as if he'd said something he shouldn't. And, yes, the girl looked... very thoughtful.

Thony knew his own eyes were wide with the idea that there people whose job seemed to be to deal with evil wizards. Whether he was more disturbed by how *freaking cool* that job was or by *how many* evil wizards there had to be to make that even a Thing... was perhaps up for debate.

Later. Debate *later*. And possibly an internal, *silent* debate. Although the look on Amanita's face suggested it might be a debate they could have *together* because she hadn't known about this either.

"I have to go," Puck repeated as if trying to convince himself, "But it's a dereliction of my responsibilities to you two – especially you," he nodded to Amanita.

Amanita shook her own head. "Don't worry about us. We'll be fine. I traveled around all on my own for several months over a year ago. I'm older now. And Thony and I are together. And everyone thinks he's a unicorn-maiden. We'll be fine."

Thony twitched his skirts. "Yeah, we'll be fine. That was the whole point of me wearing this get up, right?"

Puck was still eyeing them worriedly. "You should be, but for the sake of all those anxious, over-protective grown-ups who care about yo– *us*... stay in this room, okay? I told the innkeeper that you're my cousins – that I'm escorting you across Brelsin to an enclave of unicorns in Selavan because you, Thony were Chosen recently. And you, Amanita, were hoping to try out at the school for bards out there, so you came along."

Amanita laughed. It sounded a little forced. "I hope they don't ask me to sing or anything. Daffyd always said I sounded like a dead cow."

Puck smiled a bit distractedly. "I said the family is all hoping they'll let you down gently."

Thony folded his arms with a frown. "You want us to stay in this room? For how long? And what about the equines?"

"I paid for stabling for Twinklestar and Silverfoot," the fairy-prince said. "And food to be brought up here for you, though of course you'll go down to check on them. It should just be a couple of days... but I paid for a week, just in case." He was looking towards the door with a sense of growing impatience. "And the wards I set in here should last twice that long. I'll take them down when we leave, of course, but you should be perfectly safe in here. In fact, hardly anyone should even notice you exist if you stay in here."

Because the huge unicorn in the stable wouldn't be noticed at *all,* Thony thought. But clearly Puck needed to get going...

"We don't look enough alike to be kin," Amanita pointed out.

Puck shook his head. "Thony and I are both pale enough to be from the same area – there's redheads mixed in with blondes all along this part of the world, ever since the *Líonar* got kicked out of Pathremir." Amanita's lips went tight the way they had that other time when she'd talked about holding a grudge against people for something that happened a couple thousand years ago. So maybe '*Líonar*' was the name of those people. "And I may have hinted that your mother is from the

Muana, Amanita. The Desert reaches far enough north over here that it's not all *that* unusual to find darker-skinned people. And then there's Darjil, which seems to have had a similar seed-population to your people. And the Pardasians, for that matter."

More people and places that Thony had never heard of.

Maybe he could break Puck's stricture regarding staying in the room long enough to go buy a *map*...

Whatever it was, Amanita seemed satisfied – if slightly bemused – with his answer.

"I *really* have to go," Puck said tightly. "Stay safe, okay, you guys? I swear, I'll keep this as short a trip as I can. Lady Opalsinger is supposed to have people waiting for my report..."

"Go do what you have to do," Amanita told him again. "We'll be fine."

Puck nodded and stood up. "I don't want to have to explain to your grandmother how you died, Amanita. Or my *other* Aunt. Or my mother."

Amanita waved the fairy-man away. "Will you stop that? Just go already."

Puck gave them one last, worried look and ducked out the door.

They waited in silence for a long moment, watching the door. Thony was half-expecting him to come dashing back in and tell them that he was going to take them with him after all. It hadn't passed *his* attention that neither Amanita – nor he himself – had actually promised to stay in the room.

Had Puck forgotten to make them do so?

Or was this one of those 'trickster's honor' things he'd told them about when relating tales of all the ways he and the Eyolan God of Mischief, Destren, had turned things topsy-turvy?

It hadn't passed the young prince's attention either that Puck had referred to Amanita's people as 'her' people and not 'our' people. Nor that he'd seemed to think that her grandmother *(and which would that be? The awful one or the over-protective one?)* would be calling him to account if anything happened to the girl. And that the woman had both the right and the ability to do so... and he'd mentioned *his* mother and some 'other' Aunt – than the Fairy Queen, presumably – but not Amanita's parents. Wouldn't her *parents* be upset if she died?

Which all said something right there, although Thony wasn't sure exactly *what.*

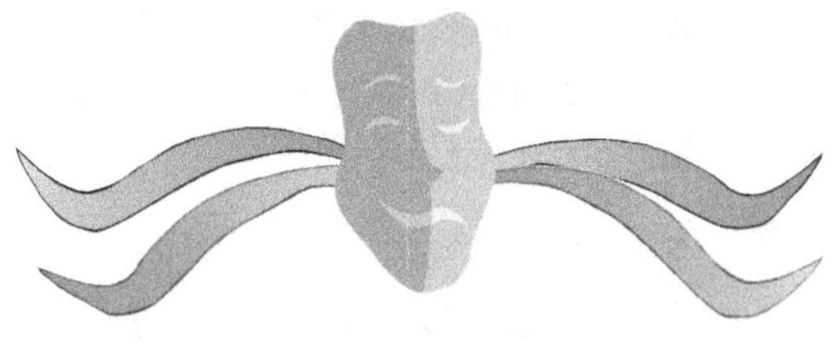

Chapter THIRTEEN

Epilogue

A SMALL TAPPING ON THE door proved to be nothing more terrifying than the innkeeper's nine-year-old son bearing a heavy tray with dinner. They took it and latched the door behind him.

Dinner proved to be a thick stew of tasteless and unidentifiable vegetables and hardrolls that were hard enough for Thony to wonder if he was going to break a tooth on one of them. It wasn't *terrible,* once they soaked the rolls in the stew for awhile, but compared to Puck and Amanita's cooking in the Fairy Wood – and the literally *royal* meals he was used to at home – it was pretty disappointing.

But Thony was a growing boy *(current outfit notwithstanding)* and it was food after a very long day. He devoured his portion and eyed Amanita's with ill-concealed longing. *(He knew it was ill-concealed, because a bit over halfway through, she rolled her eyes and shoved her bowl over to him.)*

"I guess we should check on the equines now," Thony commented when he was done at last. "Twinklestar *feels* like he's fine, but I'd like to see for myself."

"He doesn't talk to you in words?" Amanita asked curiously.

Thony shook his head. "Feelings mostly. Some images. Somehow, I seem to *know* what words he'd probably use, but there aren't any."

"Hunh." She looked thoughtful... and perhaps a bit mollified.

Though why *she* should need to be mollified might be up for some debate. It was Thony wearing this dress they both loathed.

"Yeah, we should definitely check on them." Amanita rubbed her hands together with an almost-certainly-intentional expression of maniacal glee. "And *then* we check out the rest of the town."

Thony eyed her warily. "Puck said we should stay here."

He wasn't an over-cautious boy *(in his own opinion anyways)* but he rather thought that wandering around in the dark in an unfamiliar town *(which* **he** *would have called a* **city,** *it being at least ten times larger than the village near his parents' castle)* that was occupied by the hostile forces of an evil wizard *(which was the sort of thing he suspected might be more interesting in the abstract)* just *might* be edging over into recklessness.

Amanita rolled her eyes. "Of course, he did. He had to. He's supposed to be the 'adult' in the situation. But do you think he thought we actually would do it? I mean, he *knows* us."

That... was true...

Still...

"How much are we likely to discover in the dark? Won't everyone be indoors and asleep?"

"Hmmn." That appeared to give Amanita some pause. "I was thinking we could go up on the roofs and listen through the chimneys and stuff."

Or... maybe it hadn't.

Literally eavesdropping sounded pretty cool to Thony, too. But there were practical considerations.

"I don't think I could do that much climbing tonight," he admitted. "Not after riding like I did all day. If you have any more of that arnica stuff in the saddlebags... I will *probably* be up for it tomorrow. And we could check out the town tomorrow in daylight, find out where the important buildings are, do a more targeted approach."

Amanita thought about that for a minute.

"All right," she said with a little sigh. "I guess that makes sense. Darn, but I want to get started right away, though," she added with some disappointment.

"Yeah," Thony was not about to admit his own trepidation about the situation. It was a new world, after all. Just how small Aldyrwald was had been driven home to him just during the ride in to Flowerdust. He'd just have to amp up his game was all.

At least there was *no bloody way* he could climb around rooftops in this *dress*.

Tomorrow sounded better and better.

He trailed Amanita out the door, trying to emulate his mother's most timid ladies-in-waiting. *Demure* and *modest* was what unicorn-maidens were supposed to be, Puck had said. He could fake that.

And it helped with restraining his impulse to rub his hands together with a maniacal grin as Amanita had done.

He was a prince, after all. Cackling in anticipatory glee was not Proper Princely Behavior.

But, oh! Tomorrow was going to be *fun*.

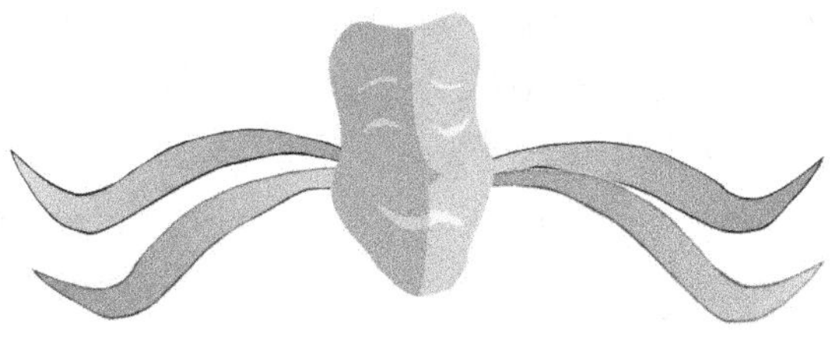

P.S.

DAE GOLDENEYES RODE INTO THE small town on the plains with one eye over her shoulder as always.

It was late enough at night that she'd probably thrown off her pursuer. They would have assumed she'd done the sensible things and made a cold camp a dozen miles back when it started to get dark.

On the other hand, they knew her.

The town – Flowerdust, if she remembered her last look at the maps right – was shut up pretty tightly. It wasn't even three hours to midnight yet, but there wasn't a single person on the streets. Well, except for that patrol of soldiers that she had dodged without half-trying, even on her horse. Of course, they'd sounded – and *smelled* – pretty drunk.

What were soldiers doing in Flowerdust anyways? It was just a dusty little town with nothing really going for it. A good place to hide, since no one in their right mind came here, but not for much else. Boring City. Yawn Capitol.

The world's youngest *(ever)* and smallest *(possibly, though there might be dwarves or something beating her out)* mercenary regarded the closed-down town with bemusement. She needed a place to stable her horse and to sleep the night away... but if even the inns and taverns were shut down for the night...

Not that she had any money left to pay for lodging for herself or her horse. Running away took a great many resources, but gave one precious little time to rebuild them. At least she had some food left in her packs.

She saw a pair of kids come out of what looked like the stables attached to an inn. They were making expressions of disgust and took great care to use the boot-scraper at the inn's front door. The taller one was wearing a long white dress – like a *proper* unicorn-maiden, unlike Dae's friend, Kamauri. But she moved wrong, somehow. Dae had been trained to notice these things at Sonoro's School of Soldiering after all. The other one was dressed in pants and a tunic and her short hair fluffed out to the sides.

"Twinklestar is never going to forgive me," the taller girl said as they entered the inn. Her hair was awfully short – almost as short as Dae's own, or the other girl's – but it caught all the firelight that briefly shone through the door; it was a brighter red than Dae had seen for some time. She must be new at this unicorn-maiden gig – Dae had sort of unintentionally kept tabs on who had been Chosen, mostly because Kamauri gave her updates as she got word. There weren't any unicorn-maidens with hair that bright red to Dae's knowledge. Or, well, there *hadn't* been. Clearly there was one *now*.

The girl's unicorn-friend must be inside the stable. So, it would be a safe place.

Once the pair of them had the inn's door securely closed behind them, Dae and her horse sneaked across the street and into the stable. The stable-door had squeaked crazily when the other kids had closed it, but Dae still had a few good bladders of oil with her and could fix that right off.

The inside of the stable was as disgusting as she had guessed, given the kids' reactions. Dae decided not to light her little thief's lantern almost immediately *(acquired at some expense, and to Kamauri's intense disapproval... but it had been required equipment for her classes on Advanced Sneaking. Really. And Kamauri... had* **sort of** *believed that).* She didn't need to see if this place actually looked worse than it smelled – not in any detail anyways.

And besides, the unicorn was sort of glowing.

Enough to see where she was going, anyways.

Enough to see where the pitchfork and shovel were, and the pile of clean(ish) hay. Enough to clean up a stall for Sandy and for herself to curl up in the back.

Her horse settled right in with some water and a scoop of the oats she found in an open sack in the back behind the clean hay. But Dae was still too keyed up to sleep.

And there was nothing else to *do,* and she sort of owed the innkeeper for stabling and the oats...

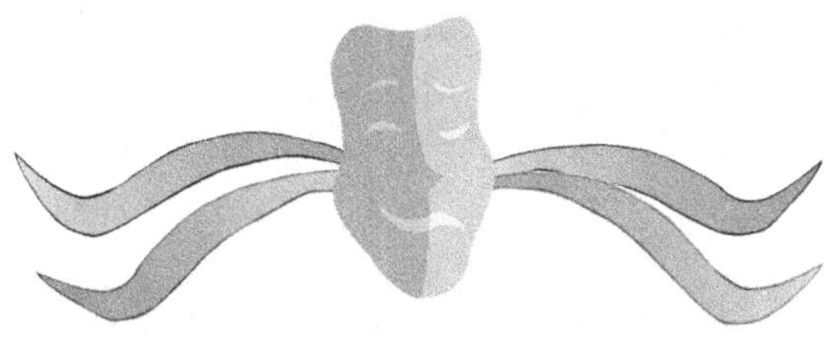

P.P.S.

"SHALLADRA THINKS I HAVE A girl in the town." The man's voice was tense. "I don't know who told her. Or who told her to check in the Inn of the Starred Hoof, but she's coming here tomorrow night. You need to leave. *Now.*"

"What? And leave her to have her soldiers create some havoc for the innkeeper when she doesn't find me here?" The woman who answered him had a musical voice that was completely unconcerned. "I've done nothing wrong, Istevan. Even the Commander of the Garrison can't arrest me for nothing at all. Not *yet* anyways."

"Julanna... Fine." The tense man clearly gave up on trying to convince *her,* and chose a different tactic. "Dav, can you at least take the baby somewhere safe?"

A hesitation, and then another man said slowly, "That makes sense..."

"She's still nursing, Istevan," the woman objected. "And Shalladra won't turn out the inn once we put on a little show for her down in the commonroom. They'll be fine up here."

"Julanna..."

The woman chuckled. "The whole point of being a *spy,* my dear, is to act nonchalant when they think they have you in their sights. You wanted to be part of this. Can you still do your part?"

The tense man heaved a sigh. "Yes..."

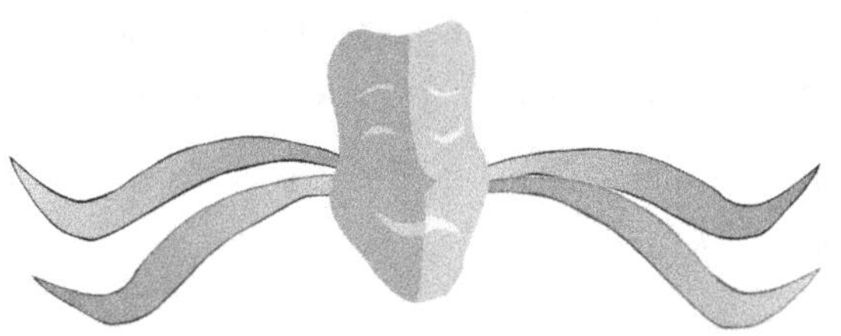

P.P.P.S.

VALDERON RAVEN'SWING SPLAYED HIS WELL-MANICURED hands out to smooth the papers neatly placed on his desk. "Flowerdust, you say?"

The messenger crouched fearfully on the floor before him nodded. "Aye, milord."

The wizard leaned back in his chair, thoughtfully stroking his smooth chin. "And you say Shalladra doesn't know?"

"No, milord. Not that I could tell, milord."

"Very good," Valderon remarked, more to himself than the messenger. "*Very* good."

Shalladra was a competent administrator – ruthless and dedicated to, well, to *himself*. As he'd been careful to ensure. *Love spell* sounded so much better than *geas*. Or *compulsion spell*. Didn't it?

But such things had the potential to backfire... now.

"You may go," he told the messenger – the *spy*. "Return to Flowerdust and keep an eye on the woman for me."

The messenger scuttled out of the room backwards, keeping to his hands and knees.

Valderon hardly noticed.

His attention was caught instead by the flower suspended under its glass cover on his desk. A silver rose it was, rotating gently as it always did. Were the petals just slightly turning to brown?

He frowned, and leaned forwards to peer at it more closely.

No. The *preservation* spell he'd set was still working. There was still time.

Time to do as he'd promised her.

Time to conquer the universe and lay it at her feet.

Time to make sure he knew where she was so that he could actually do that.

Smartly, the sorcerer stood, dusting off his hands. There were things to be set into motion if he intended to leave for Flowerdust in the morning.

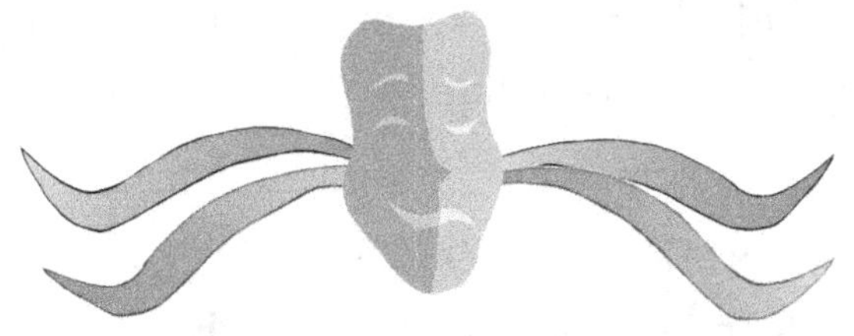

Index of Characters

- **Amanita**. A foreign girl who used to work in the castle kitchens, and most recently worked in the stables. She says she came from another world beyond the Fairy Wood.
- **Annabel** (Queen Annabel of Aldyrwald). Wife of King Bill; mother of Joanna, Priscilla, and Thony. Youngest of seven sisters and three brothers.
- **Aspenheart**, Lord. Prince of the Light-elves, an attendant of the Fairy Queen
- **Bill** (King Bill / King William Devinthal of Aldyrwald). Husband of Queen Annabel. Father of Joanna, Priscilla, and Thony. Oldest of seven brothers.
- **Dae Goldeneyes**. Youngest mercenary ever.
- **Daffyd**. Amanita's brother.
- **Dav**. An associate of Julanna.
- **David**. Son of the Chief Cook in the Aldyrwald royal kitchens. Something of a genius at making soups. (Amanita calls him 'Mr. Make-the-Stew').
- **Destren**. The Eyolan God of Mischief.
- **Eddie** (Great-Uncle Sir Eddie / Prince Edward of Aldyrwald). A middle-born brother of King Bill's father, Grandpa Tom. Thony's riding master.

- Eswith (Master Eswith). Protocol master of the Aldyrwald royal family.
- **Girona** Starshine. A student wizard from Happy-Go-Lucky on Eyola, cousin to Midele.
- **Golden Sphinx**. A Goddess on Eyola.
- **Herush**. Midele's father, Girona's uncle.
- **Istevan**. A spy helping Julanna.
- **Jeremy**. Centaur male. Husband of Priscilla. Son of Caspar and Mariah.
- **Joanna** (Princess Joanna Devinthal the Wise and Wonderful). Eldest-born princess of Aldyrwald. Daughter of King Bill and Queen Annabel; sister of Priscilla and Thony. Wife of Prince Sir Roger. Goddess of the Earth.
- **Julanna**. A woman spying on Valderon Raven'sWing's forces in Flowerdust. She has a nursing baby.
- **Lilysong**. The Fairy Queen.
- Linden. A dryad. Wife of Herush, mother of Midele, aunt to Girona.
- **Louis** (Uncle Louis / Prince Louis of Aldyrwald). King Bill's youngest brother (last of seven). Prince-consort of a coastal country.
- **Midele Featherspray**. A novice priestess of the Golden Sphinx on Eyola, Girona's cousin.
- Naeel. Amanita's father.
- **Opalsinger**, Lady. Princess of the Dark-elves, attendant of the Fairy Queen.
- **Paul**. Journeyman pastry chef in the Aldyrwald royal kitchens. (Amanita calls him 'Mr. Grabby-Hands')

- **Priscilla** (Princess Priscilla Devinthal the Bright-Eyed and Bushy-Tailed, aka Prissy). Second-born princess of Aldyrwald. Daughter of King Bill and Queen Annabel; sister of Joanna and Thony. Wife of Jeremy. Goddess of Animals (including humans) and of Love/Fertility.
- **Puck**. The 'king of pranksters', a fairy attendant of Queen Lilysong.
- **Quellarie**. Someone who advised Amanita.
- **Richie** (King Richie of Schwannsberg). Husband of Queen Janet. Father of Prince Raymond, Prince Sir Roger, Prince Ryan, Princess Laura, Princess Sophia, and Princess Tessa.
- **Roger** (Prince of Schwannsberg and Knight). Second-born son of King Richie and Queen Janet; younger brother of Prince Raymond and Princess Laura; older brother of Prince Ryan, Princess Sophia, and Princess Tessa. Husband of Joanna. God of Air.
- **Rosie**. Thony's tired old mare.
- **Sandy**. Dae Goldeneyes' horse.
- **Shalladra**. Valderon Raven'sWing's Commander of the Guard in Flowerdust.
- **Silverfoot**. Thony's rather-too-energetic horse.
- **Snackers**. Girona's pet mouse.
- **Snowmistral**. Queen of the Snow-fairies, Puck's mother.
- **Tad/Thaddeus**. Stablemaster to Aldyrwald Castle, Amanita's boss.
- **Thony** (Prince Anthony Devinthal the Affable and the Affirmative). Crown Prince of Aldyrwald. Younger brother of Princess Joanna and Princess Priscilla.

- **Twinklestar.** Unicorn, friend of Thony and Amanita.
- Valderon **Raven'sWing.** An Evil Wizard.
- **Wesley** (Wes). Stableboy in the Aldyrwald royal stables.
- **Ytheril.** Amanita's mother.

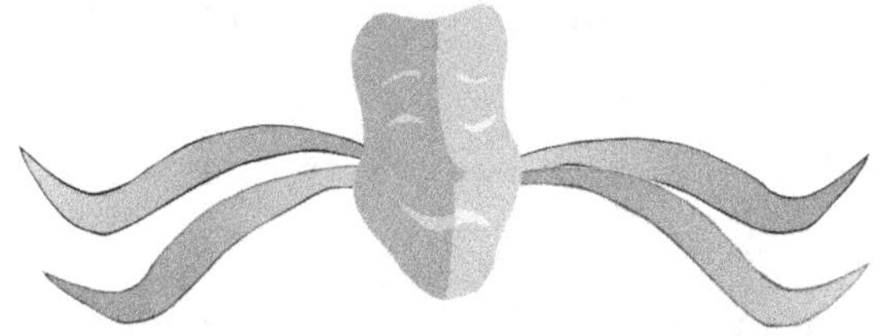

Index of Places

- **Aldyrwald**. The country where Thony is Crown Prince. Three linked valleys, centrally located in the mountain region.
- **Brelsin**. A country in the plains that regularly gets overrun by invaders. On Amanita's homeworld. East of Pathremir, Sethival, Selavan, Plains of Gavenor.
- **Dawil**. A country on Amanita's homeworld.
- **Eyola**. The world that Midele and Girona are from.
- Fairy Wood. A forest that bridges the gap between many worlds. Only the fairies and elves know how to navigate it by nature, though others can learn.
- **Flowerdust**. A small nowhere-sort of town in Brelsin.
- **Flowericka**. Midele's homeland on Eyola.
- **Happy-Go-Lucky**. Girona's homeland on Eyola.
- **Pathremir**. A country in the mountains on Amanita's homeworld.
- **Plains of Gavenor**. An area on Amanita's homeworld. West of Brelsin.
- **Quest'sEnd**. Home of Midele. Located in Flowericka on Eyola.

- **Selavan**. A country on Amanita's homeworld. West of Brelsin.
- **Sethival**. A country on Amanita's homeworld. West of Brelsin.
- **Schwannsberg.** Two valley kingdom immediately adjacent to Aldyrwald, Roger's homeland.

Also by Kerridwen Mangala McNamara

YOUNG ADULT Fiction:

- ***Thony and the Much-Anticipated Adventure***
  Book One of The Prankster Prince
- ***A Not-So-Sacrificial Maiden*** .
  Book One of the Knightess of the Realm

More YA coming soon...

- ***So You Want to Be a Hero*** .
  Book Three of the Prankster Prince

ADULT Fiction:

- ***The Rebel Duchess*** .
  Book One of the Chronicles of Ilseador
- ***A Not-So-Simple Mission*** .
  Book Two of the Knightess of the Realm
-

More Adult coming soon...

- ***The King's Champion*** .
  Book Two of the Chronicles of Ilseador
- ***A Not-So-Unexpected Problem*** .
  Book Three of the Knightess of the Realm

Non-fiction:

- ***The Homeschooling Parent*** .
  Self-care and Feeding of the Person Who Makes It All Happen

More non-fiction coming soon...

- ***The Homeschooling Parent Teaches MATH!*** .

Author's Note

If you're reading this, I have to assume that you're enjoying reading about Thony and Amanita. (And Twinklestar. We mustn't forget Twinklestar.)

It's only been about four months since I got *Thony and the Much-Anticipated Adventure* out the door (and into your hands and/or in front of your eyes), so I feel like it's very important that I say this...

...I'm probably not going to manage to get another Thony book out *every* four months. It might be slower (it might be faster) but I have other things to get done, and that's just life.

Those other things include two other book series (so far... bwa-ha-ha!), not to mention more books on homeschooling.

And, oh yeah, the four kids I am actually homeschooling IRL, aka 'fodder for my stories'.

No, Thony isn't based on any of them. (Nor are Amanita, Karana, Ivan, Kefen, Damien, Genevieve, Jason, Adam, etc., etc., etc.) With a few striking exceptions, the characters in all these stories are all themselves (or maybe parts of me) and other than the real-life stories I share in my writing about homeschooling, what makes it into the books are snippets of conversation or situations that I've watched people go through. Those snippets are just as likely to come from other places, people, TV, movies, and so on. If you know me and see something in here that you think you did... no, it's probably not you (sorry...).

The 'striking exceptions' are a few characters that are more directly inspired by certain people I knew long, long ago. But the original creation of those characters has gone far enough from the start that I can't really tag more than a few things – like certain verbal mannerisms – on those people. Which is just as well, because we all grew up and aren't much like those characters anymore anyways. If you know me and you think you know whom I'm talking about, go ahead and email me at RisingDragonBooks@gmail.com

Actually, go ahead and email me anyways – and join my newsletter so you can get updates about progress on the next Thony book (and my other projects... or ask to join the Prankster Prince newsletter and *only* get Thony updates).

About the Author

Kerridwen Mangala McNamara is an Indian-American with a Master's degree in Bacterial Genetics who lives in Flyover Country (the far northern end of the US South) with her husband, The Professor, four of her six children, and three goats. The goats eat, The Professor plays chess, and the children largely unschool while Mangala writes. (The remaining children are in college – you can blame the oldest for the excessive amounts of math showing up in Mangala's fantasy novels, the second one for better attention to staging of scenes, the third for all the economics, and the fourth for great attention to history – and all of them for a focus on political science!) Mangala is a former professional bellydance instructor, currently coaches FIRST Lego League and model government teams, runs homeschool parent support groups, and used to enjoy knitting, crotchet and embroidering Temari balls but now is much more boring as she rarely does anything but write, argue economic theory with her 17 and 14 year olds, and wonder loudly if her 11 and 9 year olds do anything other than watch Minecraft videos. She owes her love of books and reading to her mother, who was a professional folklorist and could recite – from memory – stories from every nation in the United Nations.

www.ingramcontent.com/pod-product-compliance
Lightning Source LLC
Chambersburg PA
CBHW070401200726
48294CB00003B/1035
9781960160157